M000004350

THE TRUTH OF THE ALEKE

ALSO BY MOSES OSE UTOMI

THE FOREVER DESERT SERIES

The Lies of the Ajungo

Daughters of Oduma

THE TRUTH OF THE
ALEKE

MOSES OSE UTOMI

TOR PUBLISHING GROUP
NEW YORK

This is a work of fiction. All of the characters, organizations, and events portrayed in this novella are either products of the author's imagination or are used fictitiously.

THE TRUTH OF THE ALEKE

Copyright © 2024 by Moses Ose Utomi

All rights reserved.

A Tordotcom Book
Published by Tom Doherty Associates / Tor Publishing Group
120 Broadway
New York, NY 10271

www.tor.com

Tor® is a registered trademark of Macmillan Publishing Group, LLC.

The Library of Congress Cataloging-in-Publication Data
is available upon request.

ISBN 978-1-250-84905-2 (hardback)
ISBN 978-1-250-84838-3 (ebook)

Our books may be purchased in bulk for promotional, educational, or business use. Please contact your local bookseller or the Macmillan Corporate and Premium Sales Department at 1-800-221-7945, extension 5442, or by email at MacmillanSpecialMarkets@macmillan.com.

First Edition: 2024

Printed in the United States of America

0 9 8 7 6 5 4 3 2 1

To my parents,
Oseyi Mike Utomi and Stella Odalomhen Uwaibi-Utomi,
who journeyed bravely beyond their City of Lies,
shared generously the water they found,
and prepared me for my own journey
through the Forever Desert

THE TRUTH OF THE ALEKE

THE ALEKE IS CRUEL.

This first truth was learned in the days of the Greatmamas, just as the Wellspring returned water to the world, after the fall of the evil Chief Tutu. The most powerful Seer the Goddess had ever chosen, Chief Tutu and his armies conquered the Free Cities of the Forever Desert, constructing a road from the bones of their enemies that coursed halfway around the world.

The great Ijefi, oba of the last free city, watched Chief Tutu's army emerge from the desert to surround her city's walls. Ijefi was a poet, an astronomer, a woman of culture. When Chief Tutu demanded she swear fealty, she refused.

"I am already sworn to peace."

Her final words.

Chief Tutu's army took the city within a day. Chief Tutu himself beheaded Oba Ijefi within her palace, then rolled her head down its steps. He sacked the city, then declared it to have a new name, one that mocked their pledge of peace against the inevitability of war: the City of Lies.

Yet this is only where the story begins.

Intoxicated by victory and seated proudly in his new throne room, Chief Tutu's end soon came at the hands of a single soldier—a low-rank spearman who had lost his unit in the fighting. Captured and tortured, but refusing to be broken, the soldier freed himself, wrenched a spear from a guard, and hurled it at Chief Tutu, impaling him to his throne.

Centuries passed. As Chief Tutu's empire crumbled to infighting, life flourished along the central river valley, and travelers from across the Forever Desert sought out the city, inspired by the memory of the Spearman.

It was then that the Aleke emerged.

Armored in night, a terror born from the depths of the rolling desert, he was inspired not by the valiant memory of the Spearman, but the atrocities of Chief Tutu. His followers, the Cult of Tutu, soon swelled into an army. The new cities of the Forever Desert closed their gates, sentencing the upstart conqueror to death by desert heat.

But *the Aleke is clever.*

This second truth was learned when the cities' gates were opened from within by agents of the Aleke. His cult flooded forth, sacking city after city and cutting out the tongues of all conquered peoples, so that they would forever remember the folly of revolt and forever beseech the mercy of subjugation. From then, the Aleke's Cult of Tutu grew, crushing each subsequent city with greater ease and more monstrous violence.

Soon, there was once again but a single free city standing against an evil overlord of the Forever Desert. But rather than a peaceful City of Lies, what the Aleke encountered was a city that was armed and battle ready. A city that remembered the fate of its peaceful predecessors and clung instead to the ferocious resistance of the Spearman.

The City of Truth.

For three centuries, the war between the Aleke and the City of Truth has raged. The city's walls have been destroyed, thousands of its warriors killed, its way of life endangered. Only the city's elite warriors, the Truthseekers, have kept the city from suffering the fate that so many have suffered. But the Aleke is cruel, and the Aleke is clever, and all the citizens of the City of Truth know the day is approaching when the Aleke will bring the full might of the Cult of Tutu crashing down upon the City of Truth, a final battle to end the unending war.

The Aleke is coming.

And only Osi can stop him.

PART I

1

OSI ALWAYS DREADED returning home.

Out in the city, he was Junior Peacekeeper Osi, the pride of his community. In his pale blue robes, bronze half helm, and sturdy sandals, he was the very image of the Spearman. His duty to keep the city's peace was a sacred one.

At home, he was just Osi. Washer of cutlery, sweeper of floors.

And today, he was even less than that.

"Eh heh, look at him," his mama said, surveying his busted lip and swollen right hand. "The fighter."

News of Osi's day had flown ahead of him.

"Hello, Mama," he said sheepishly, standing in the doorway, his eyes held fast to the floor.

His family was seated on the ground around a large, circular dining cloth. There were two open spaces to sit, one of which was left empty in his baba's memory. Osi went to the other spot between his two older and two younger sisters, then sat with care on his tender backside.

"Does it hurt?" his youngest sister whispered.

He shook his head. His commander had given him ten lashes for insubordination, whipping him across his butt right in the middle of Central District's most active roundabout. Pain was bearable. As was humiliation. The real punishment was far worse.

"So no Ascendance for this one," his mama said sharply. Osi could feel her eyes on him. "In the entire history of this city, you are the first ever to be disinvited. What an honor for this family. Congratulations, Osi."

The Ascendance was the biggest ceremony in the City of Truth. It was only held when it was time to induct a new class of Truthseekers, and it had been six years since the last Ascendance. The next was likely a decade away.

A once-in-a-generation event that Osi's commitment to the Peace-keepers had earned him an invitation to, despite his record of misdeeds. And he'd ruined it.

"What happened this time, eh?" his mama spat.

He took a deep breath. "Mama, they were thieves. I watched them steal from the Ihenwele bakery with my own eyes. So I chased them."

"You chased them so much you broke your hand and face?" she asked.

Beside him, his eldest sister mumbled under her breath, "Do not explain. Just apologize."

His sister was wise. Far wiser than Osi. An apology would lead to dinner, warm food in his belly, a peaceful night's rest, and sanctuary from his mama's ire.

But Osi didn't care about any of those things. The world was a place of good and evil, right and wrong. Punishing thieves for stealing from innocent citizens was right. If it was against the rules for a Junior Peacekeeper to arrest bad people, then it was the rules that needed to change, not him.

Do not fear that you may do wrong, his baba had taught him from a young age. *Fear that you may not do right.*

Osi raised his face, his eyes meeting his mama's. "I chased them and taught them never to steal again."

"Why is he this way?" His eldest sister sighed.

An argument ensued.

Osi and his mama shared a temper—the sort that simmered before inevitably boiling over. All their fights transcended the moment, dredging up unforgiven trespasses from years before, burdened by a refusal to accept the other's imperfections. To his mama, Osi bore the same impetuous foolishness that had gotten her husband killed. To Osi, his mama was too fearful and weak to imagine a better world. Neither was incorrect.

"Again and again," his mama shouted. "They have been patient with you, and this is how you behave? Disinvited from the Ascen-dance . . . Imagine! You are lucky he did not dismiss you entirely, you godsblind child!"

"Dismiss for what?" Osi shot back, earning groans from his sisters. "They were thieves! If I see bad people in our city, I will fight them and fight them and fight them and if you do not like it I DO NOT CARE!"

He was crying. He always cried when he got angry and he always got angry when he argued with his mama. Crying, chest heaving, every muscle in his body was clenched with the rage and fear and frustration of not being understood.

"And now he cries," said one of his sisters.

"Mama, may we be excused?" another asked.

His mama's rage seemed to evaporate. She beheld her son with only pity, like she was looking upon a sheep wandering the desert alone, unaware of the hunters on its trail.

"You think you are always right, Osi," she said in a calm voice. "One day you will learn you are a fool like everyone else, and that you should have listened to your betters.

"But until that day . . ." she added, locking him in a lethal gaze, "you are not six, you are sixteen. Act your age. If you bring another drop of shame on this family, I swear by the Spearman Himself that I will disown you. Do you hear?"

Osi wiped the tears from his face, but they kept coming. He wanted to rage through the house, breaking every dish and tearing down the walls. But he didn't want his little sisters to see him like that. So instead, he shot a final dark glance at his mama, turned, and stormed out the front door.

*   *   *

In the days of the Greatmamas, it was said that the city was surrounded by massive walls. But the Aleke had spent centuries tearing them down with giant machines that hurled rocks the size of a house. Now, there was no trace that the walls had ever existed. Instead, watchtowers had been raised throughout the city, allowing the Peacekeepers to both monitor the city's happenings and to watch the horizon for the approach of the Aleke and his cult.

When Osi was a child, the Aleke's raids had come often. Sometimes, the city burned. But most of the time, the Peacekeepers, his baba among them, would form up and march out to the city limits, facing the endless expanse of the Forever Desert. Led by the mighty Truthseekers, they would intercept the Aleke's forces, turning them back. Baba had died in such a fight, slain in the desert by some un-named Cultist.

But his sacrifice had not been in vain. The City of Truth still lived and was stronger than ever. The fear of the Aleke had created a sense of unity, driving crime down, bolstering the ranks of the Peacekeep-ers, and filling the city's tax coffers so as to rebuild the watchtowers at the city's farthest edges.

Osi climbed the watchtower nearest his home, an old model that was now rarely staffed. At the top, he leaned against the wooden rail-ing, taking deep breaths. To the west, the sky was slashed pink and orange as the sun lowered toward the Citadel of Truth on the hori-zon. Cascading tiers of brick homes and businesses slid toward the river and its green-lined valley. To the east, the Forever Desert was an expanse of barren, untamed sand. It mocked the city with its mirage of emptiness; just beyond the horizon, in every direction, the Aleke and the Cult of Tutu waited patiently with their sharpened teeth and blunt-cut tongues. Only a thin ring of desert separated the stable order of the city from the mad violence of the Cult. It was the only defense the city had, besides the people of the city itself.

People like Osi. He was doing his best, but some days he felt like he was the only one who really cared.

"Osi!"

He followed the sound of the voice to the base of the tower.

"Osi?" Inusu called, peering up at him.

She was his neighbor and oldest friend. They'd gone through childhood side by side and had joined the Junior Peacekeepers on the same day. Unlike Osi, though, Inusu was smart and emotion-ally sober. She'd warned him not to pursue thieves, but he hadn't listened.

Osi wiped the moisture from his cheeks and waved her up. She joined him but remained silent for a while, enjoying the city overlook.

"You heard me and Mama fighting?" he eventually asked.

She nodded. "You never close your windows. The whole neighbor-hood heard."

Osi didn't care what their neighbors thought of him. But he didn't like them thinking less of his mama, even if he was angry with her. "Did you hear what she said?" he asked.

"She would be wrong to disown you, yes," Inusu replied. "But you were disinvited from the Ascendance, Osi . . ."

She didn't need to finish. The severity was clear. The greatest honor of his life, taken away.

"What is wrong with me?" he asked.

"Too much to say."

Osi tried to laugh, but as soon as he opened his mouth, a sob came out and the tears came again and he buried his face in his hands. Inusu put a hand on Osi's shoulder.

"There will be other Ascendances," she said unconvincingly.

Of course there would be. But it didn't matter.

This Ascendance was the only one he wanted to attend. *These* Ascendants—Izen the Wise, Dikende the Mighty, Clever Hizojie, and, most of all, the Legendary Lumhen—were the ones he'd idolized since he was a boy, the finest Ascendant class in living memory. Osi had only seen them once before, the day they were introduced as Ascendants and paraded through the streets. That had been ten years ago. Since then, they'd undergone the most arduous training in the world. He'd built himself up too, following in his baba's footsteps of joining the Peacekeepers.

Osi'd always believed that if he could just see the Ascendants again, and let them see him, that maybe they'd understand his desire to better the city in a way no one else could.

Osi took a great inhale to still his shuddering chest. Crying was no use. Tomorrow, his peers would be enjoying the Ascendance. And he would be at the barracks, washing the laundry of every Peacekeeper in the city.

"I just want to do what is right," he explained.

Inusu nodded but didn't speak. And long after she'd climbed back down the watchtower and gone to bed, Osi stayed out, watching over the darkened city, praying for the day when he would finally learn from his mistakes.

It was a prayer he would soon regret.

2

OSI SCRUBBED THE INSIDE of a bronze half helm, his fingers pruned from water. Sounds of revelry floated over the barracks wall. As the city had awakened, so had the chants. So had the street singers. So had the squealing children and laughing families, all of them drunk on joy as they paraded through the city to the foot of the Citadel of Truth.

Osi couldn't help himself.

He dropped the helm into the soapy bucket and scaled the wall. Seeing the festivities was even worse than hearing them. The road was a crowded mosaic of humanity. Beaming faces, pockets of jubilant dance. The elderly lined either side of the street, perched in their rocking chairs and looking on with expressions of peaceful nostalgia. Vendors sold roasted chicken and coconut gari. Young girls tied gold and blue ribbons in their friends' hair.

It was everything he imagined. Except he had imagined himself as part of it.

Being a Junior Peacekeeper had become his entire life. He patrolled every day and trained every night. His devotion had cost him friends, to the point that his only remaining ones were Peacekeepers themselves. His work stipend was the only consistent income his family earned. All to follow in his baba's footsteps.

But he was more than just a Junior Peacekeeper, much as the Spearman had been more than just a spearman. Most people believed history was the story of other people, but Osi knew better. History was the story of those worth writing about.

He was meant to be at the Ascendance.

Spearman, guide me.

Before Osi realized what he was doing, he was sliding down the other side of the wall and running as hard as he'd ever run in his life. He sped down narrow streets, maneuvering around celebrants and vendors, until he reached a throng of citizens pooled before the imposing figure of the Citadel of Truth.

A million fist-sized stones, carefully stacked and sealed together, coagulated into an impregnable fortress that soared five stories high. Twin banners, each bearing a gold Spearman on a blue field, draped down its exterior. Wooden pilasters poked out from its square central tower.

The Ascendance would take place atop that tower. From the ground, if the assembly was silent, they would perhaps be able to hear the ceremony. But they wouldn't see anything until the very end, when the Ascendants walked over to the edge to wave to the onlookers.

Osi had to get closer.

He waded through the crowd and reached the Citadel's arched entrance, only to run straight into two Peacekeepers.

"Osi?" one of the guards asked, eyebrow raised. Osi didn't recognize him. "Are you sick in your mind?"

"I am on orders," was all Osi said in a low, dire tone, continuing past them without slowing. "I will explain later."

The Peacekeeper seemed entirely unconvinced. He raised an incredulous eyebrow and moved to stand in Osi's way. But his more senior comrade stalled him.

"Leave him be," he said. "If he is lying, we will get to see the boy whipped again."

And Osi was in the Citadel of Truth.

He rushed down cold hallways, past flawless portraits of all the city's historical leaders and the obas who ruled in the days of the Greatmamas—including a portrait of the great Oba Ijefi with her cloud of white hair and humble beggar's clothing. He flew up the central staircase, then crouched against the short wall at the top, ears straining to hear through the gentle shifting of the rooftop wind.

". . . a sacred rite. As children, these Ascendants swore a vow to the City of Truth, to devote their lives to its defense."

The top of the Citadel was an empty terrace of gray stone but for a narrow residence on the far side with two heavy golden doors. In front of those golden doors was a throne fashioned from rare black wood, in front of which stood a figure shrouded in a floor-length black khaftan, a blue cap atop their head.

The Speaker.

They were the voice of the city itself, the spiritual descendant of the Spearman. They were elevated by the city's Elders, imbued with authority even higher than the Truthseekers. Over their face was a bronze mask that concealed their identity, shielding them from the impurities and political machinations of the city's wealthy.

Osi noticed that there was no gap for him in the ranks of the Junior Peacekeepers. That underscoring of his insignificance wounded him as much as being disinvited. He bitterly noted that none of them were even doing their duty properly. All of the Peacekeepers were watching the ceremony rather than scanning for threats.

All except Inusu. Her eyes widened as she saw Osi.

As the Speaker proceeded with the ceremony, their voice carrying across the roof, Inusu mouthed words at Osi.

What are you doing?

I had to see it! he mouthed back.

Inusu's shock morphed, brows turning down, lips pursing.

Pity.

It was the same pity Osi had seen on his mama's face, and seeing it on the face of his best friend made him realize how foolish he was being. He was acting without thinking again, just as he had when chasing the thieves.

What is wrong with me? he wondered.

Inusu's eyes gave him sage advice. *Leave, Osi. Please.*

This was a dismissal-worthy offense. If anyone other than Inusu saw him, he would lose his uniform, lose his authority to patrol, lose his stipend and the ability to feed his family.

But his desire to see the Truthseekers—to experience proximity to greatness—was stronger, as most things were, than his sense. He crept forward, peeking out past the stairway wall.

There they were. Each still in the red robes of the Ascendant rather than Truthseeker gold. Fewer than twenty strides away from him.

Izen the Wise. She was slender, with dark puffs under her eyes and thin hair that was cut haphazardly at her shoulders. It was said she never slept, and Osi could see immediately where that rumor came from. But despite her exhausted appearance, she had an air of unconcern, as if even in her tired state, she knew there was nothing she was unprepared for.

Dikende the Mighty. He was easily the biggest man Osi had ever seen. His muscles looked like wet, black cloths that had been wrung and wrung and wrung until they were completely devoid of moisture, tight enough to chip stone. Unlike Izen's aloofness, Dikende was alert, his attention shifting like a bird's from one point to another.

Clever Hizojie. The spill of short braids at the back of his shaved head and his heavily tattooed right arm made him one of the most recognizable Ascendants. Unlike his peers, Hizojie had grown up an orphan in the city's Sunrise District, the main site of the Cult's raids. The experience had forged him into a man as careful and lethal as a blade between the ribs. His eyes held a persistent skepticism, like reality was a puzzle he was on the verge of solving.

Lastly, there was Lumhen.

Osi's heart double-drummed as he watched her stand, bathed in sunlight. There was so much to notice about her—the dark umber of her skin against the crimson of her robes; her leggy, athletic frame; her upright and regal posture. But all Osi could see was her smile. While the other Ascendants seemed in some way subdued by the solemnness of the moment, Lumhen seemed above it. The gentle curve of her lips demonstrated why—despite Izen's calm, Dikende's ferocity, and Hizojie's sly charisma—Lumhen was the face of this class of Ascendants. She was the embodiment of love, hope, confidence. She was also the most powerful Seer in five hundred years, rumored to be more powerful than Chief Tutu himself.

At just twenty years old, she was already a legend.

A group of Peacekeepers carried over a golden chest and held it out before the Truthseekers. Inside were little black balls that could have been jewelry beads if they so clearly weren't. They were unnaturally smooth, and their color wasn't simply black—they seemed to suck in light and destroy it, a darkness deeper than any other.

These were the God's Eyes, Osi knew. Ancient and powerful artifacts that were the city's main hope against the Aleke and his Cultists. But the chest wasn't even half full, maybe thirty beads in all. Once, there had been hundreds of God's Eyes in the city's possession, and as many

Truthseekers to wield them. But each time a Truthseeker was killed or captured by the Aleke, that was one God's Eye that couldn't be recovered. Over time, the city's stock had dwindled.

Each Ascendant took a God's Eye, raised it in a closed fist, and saluted—left arm bent behind their backs in a gesture of peace, right fist tapping the heart, then upright against the shoulder like a spear, ready to fight against evil as the Spearman had. Then they recited the Three Truths.

"The Aleke is cruel," they recited. "The Aleke is clever. The Aleke is coming."

They each popped the stones into their mouths, swallowing them down without the slightest grimace.

Then, suddenly, Lumhen turned her head from the Speaker and looked directly at him.

Osi froze beneath her gaze, grappling with its impossibility. How could she be looking at him? But it wasn't just Lumhen. Hizojie and Dikende and Izen. The Peacekeepers too. Even the Speaker. They were all staring right at him.

"I . . ." he began. "Good morning . . ."

No, not *at* him. *Past* him.

Osi turned.

High in the sky, above the endless desert, a dark star rose. None of them understood what they were seeing—a shadowed mass floating up toward the sun. The way bits of it crumbled and drifted to the earth made it seem like it was made of sand. But that didn't make any sense. How could there be sand in the sky?

As the mass passed in front of the sun, its shadow fell over the Citadel. An uncertain murmur rose from the crowd in the plaza below.

A wonder brimming with confusion.

Then confusion turning to fear.

And then, as the mass descended toward them with air-rending speed, fear became a dry-mouthed terror.

The Juniors panicked, some rushing toward Peacekeepers for protection and others running for the stairs, creating a jam that immediately became a crushing stampede.

The Ascendants all stared up in disbelief. Except for Izen the Wise.

Her eyes narrowed in determination as she raised her hands toward the descending ball.

Then her skin sparkled with the power of the God's Eye. Each pore glinted like glass, refracting a dull iridescence.

Osi had faith that nothing was too much for these Ascendants. But as the mass drew closer and he began to understand how large it was, he couldn't help but remember his argument with his mama. How senseless and hurtful it had been for the both of them. He prayed that he would see her again, to apologize. To perhaps give her a hug and kiss and let her know that, though he was a fool now, he wouldn't be a fool forever.

Then there was a low roar of sound, followed immediately by the world breaking. The floor liquefied, up became down, and Osi's thoughts were silenced.

3

OSI COUGHED HIMSELF back to consciousness. Around him was all dark and rubble, the groans of the injured and urgent calls of the healthy. Above him, a crumble of the stone ceiling yielded to open sky, a beam of light falling through. There, looming in the sunlight with their backs to Osi, the four Ascendants stood unblemished and resplendent in their red robes.

Even then, without the benefit of foresight, Osi understood it to be a moment that would define his life. Something was wrong. And above him, less than a hundred paces away, the Truthseekers were preparing to right it.

And he could be there beside them.

"I have to help," he said to no one in particular.

He was on his feet, climbing up juts of collapsed stone.

"Osi!" Inusu cried from below. "Where are you going?"

"I am going to help them!" he said.

"Osi, look around, we need you here!"

But he was already atop the crumbled Citadel.

"It is a trap," Lumhen was saying. Osi had never heard her voice before. It was warm bread dipped in honey. "Only engage if you must. I will escort the Speaker to safety."

"Understood," the others responded.

For a moment, Lumhen stood looking out over the city, her long, single braid carrying on the breeze like a battle flag. Then, she turned away from her comrades and crossed the terrace. As she did, she noticed Osi and favored him with a soft smile, her dimpled cheeks freezing him, setting him ablaze. There was no reason to worry, the smile said. There was nothing Lumhen couldn't handle.

She opened the two golden doors to the house atop the Citadel and ushered the Speaker inside.

Osi looked back to the other Truthseekers.

"This is disgusting," Clever Hizojie said.

"Be calm, Hizo," said Izen the Wise.

Osi didn't understand what they were talking about. He moved over to join them on the edge of the Citadel so he could see what they were seeing.

What he saw was a nightmare.

The entire front face of the Citadel of Truth was demolished. Stone had been blasted in every direction, and where there had been battlements and windows and interior rooms, there was now bare, crumbled chaos. Down in the plaza in front of the Citadel, hundreds of corpses were scattered about, each broken in its own particular way. A twisted neck here, a split torso there. One body a red smear, one blue and bloated. Most of them, more than he could count, were just crushed. Flattened. As if their bones had forgotten what bones do.

Osi had never seen a dead person before. They were so still. *Why can they not move?* he thought. Some still had heads and legs, but they were just as gone as the others. He wondered if his baba had looked that way once, body intact but spirit departed.

Among all that death, there were still the living. Hundreds of survivors, some too injured to flee, some refusing to leave the injured behind, others dazed by fear.

Then, from the east, emerging from a line of shops and homes, came a monster. It was an enormous man, of a size with Dikende, atop an equally enormous camel. Clad in a boiled hippo leather overcoat with bronze half-moon rings rippling down its front, his head was hidden by a wickedly carved helm with a single horn protruding from it. In his hands was a massive war scythe with a crescent blade, held so casually and confidently that Osi felt cold at the thought of what the beast could do with it.

The monster was flanked by a half dozen warriors on either side. Thin and hard, every one of them, with an almost trancelike emptiness in the face. Their short, straight blades shone sickly in the sunlight.

Osi knew what he was seeing. But his mind did not accept it until Clever Hizojie put words to his fear.

"The Aleke has come."

* * *

The Aleke's Cultists strode forward into the plaza and calmly buried their blades between any eyes that still blinked. The sounds of the massacre rode the wind, drifting to the top of the Citadel, where Osi felt the first true fear he'd ever felt in his life.

Then the Peacekeepers began their counterattack. They emerged from the rubble, securing leather bands around their wrists, each with a single God's Eye embedded in it. Short swords sliding out of scabbards and pale blue robes aglow, they leapt down several levels of stone to the plaza floor. There, they bravely met their foes, the two lines clashing. Bronze met bronze, blade met blade; blocks and parries, quick slashes and careful thrusts.

And then they began to die. Peacekeeper after Peacekeeper, men and women in their primes, fell to the superior skill and vicious barbarity of the Cultists. In short time, their innards littered the plaza.

"I am going," Hizojie said with a hard face.

"As am I," Dikende agreed, his voice as mountainous as he was.

"Inadvisable," Izen responded coolly, eyes focused on the battlefield. "Lumhen is correct in her analysis. He is waiting for our engagement so he can flank us. Let the Peacekeepers fulfill their role."

"While citizens die," Hizojie countered, tightening his robes. "Go, Diki. I am with you."

Dikende's skin erupted with light, as if the sun were trapped beneath it. He hopped down from the Citadel roof in a single bound, cracking the stone floor of the plaza as he landed.

He charged and met the Cultists head on, plowing into and through them as their entire line collapsed on him from all sides. The clatter of bronze against bronze was gone, replaced with thuds, snaps, and squelches as flesh and bone were destroyed. Unarmored and unarmed, he savaged them. Their frantic slashes bounced harmlessly off his skin as the Peacekeepers fell back, dragging their wounded away from the violence and staring in awe as one man was doing what an entire unit of them couldn't.

"This is folly," Izen chided. "The city needs Truthseekers more than it does Peacekeepers. He puts himself at risk."

"For good cause," Hizojie said, scanning the fray.

But Izen was right. Two Cultists who had remained in reserve raised blow flutes to their lips. Slips of reflected sunlight shot out of each, striking Dikende. Osi thought they would bounce off Dikende again, just like the swords had.

Instead, Dikende flinched as the first one sank into his skin, then reeled as the second slammed home as well. At that moment, the attackers near Dikende dropped their bronze swords and drew short, iron daggers.

"No . . ." Izen mumbled.

Hizojie released a haggard scream, his skin flaring with light as he leapt from the top of the Citadel.

Most citizens of the city knew little about Seeing, but everyone knew that iron was the one thing the Goddess couldn't See. For this reason, the metal had been banned from the city for hundreds of years and its pale silver color evoked fear at a glance. An iron blade could hurt a Seer like it would anyone else, a truth even Chief Tutu had succumbed to.

As Dikende the Mighty staggered, slices of wet blood gleaming on his skin as the Cultists pursued him, the broken stone floor of the plaza began to clatter from the rumble of a charging camel. Izen screamed Hizo's name, a startling outburst from the otherwise quiet Truthseeker. Hizo, charging to defend Dikende, drew up short, eyes widening.

The Aleke burst into the fray. He raised his moon-bladed scythe above him with both arms, then brought it down in a vicious cut that blasted through Dikende's skull, a spray of bone and brain washing across the plaza.

Just like that, Dikende the Mighty was dead.

The Aleke is clever.

Hizojie staggered back and let out a cry of such bottomless heartbreak that no words could fill it. Izen fell silent, as if the blow had ended her as well.

Osi couldn't breathe.

What is happening?

Tears streamed down his cheeks, his nose stuffy against the stench of blood, his chest shaking from shallow breaths. What an embarrassing death his would be—terrified, weeping, and useless, a victim of his own poor judgment.

That was when he saw it sitting on the floor beside him. A round, black ball the size of a coin, perfectly smooth. A God's Eye. It must have fallen out of the chest in all the chaos. Just a moment before, in what already seemed like a different lifetime, he'd watched the Ascendants swallow them whole. This little black ball was the key to the power of the Truthseekers.

Osi had always known he was destined to do something great. But until this moment, ambitious as he was, he never imagined that he would be the one to end the reign of the Aleke.

Do not fear that you may do wrong. Fear that you may not do right.

Osi listened to Baba and to his fear, picked up the God's Eye, and put it into his mouth.

*   *   *

Both hands on his neck, Osi squeezed desperately, hoping to change the shape of his throat to help the God's Eye down. It didn't work. His heart pumped in his ears and black tendrils crept into his vision. His legs weakened, and he fell to his back just hard enough for the God's Eye to dislodge and slide down into his stomach.

Every pore, every hair, every fold and wrinkle on his body felt impaled on a fiery spear, and for a long moment the pain wiped all thoughts from his mind. A void. Neither dead nor alive, just empty. He floated in that void for a second of disintegrated bliss before all of reality crashed into him at once.

All of it.

Places he'd never been, people he'd never seen, words that weren't words, and living buildings made of sand; men in strange red clothes and women in white; rivers empty and full, a forest the size of the whole world; an old man with strong forearms and no fear in his heart; a frail boy with sad eyes that hid an insatiable bloodlust; war and war and war, with lives extinguished like wind-blown candles; the whole world like a child's ball spinning in a black void, other worlds doing the same in the distance.

Then it was gone, replaced by the single, stable reality of the Citadel of Truth around him. He was on his back, staring up at the sky. He raised an arm and it was sparkling, a million points of dull light shining out of his pores.

He climbed back to his feet and looked again over the plaza.

Hizojie and Izen were at the foot of the Citadel. A half ring of Cultists advanced toward them, pinning them against a wall. Behind his Cultists, the Aleke was pacing his mount, looking around impatiently, waiting for something.

Osi stamped a foot, testing his newfound strength. Maybe he wasn't a trained Truthseeker, but he was a Seer now. More important, he was determined.

He descended the shattered face of the Citadel, his hands immune to the sharp, jagged stone poking out of it. *Spearman, protect me*, he thought to himself a dozen times. *Spearman, protect me, Spearman, protect me.*

Once he reached the plaza floor, he turned toward the battle. The Cultists were nearing their targets. Then there was the Aleke, death upon camelback. *The Aleke is coming.* He'd heard it his entire life. *The Aleke is coming.* Centuries of preparation, yet when the Aleke had come, the city hadn't been ready.

But Osi was.

He sprinted across the plaza, not breaking stride as he scooped up a fallen Cultist's iron blade, eyes locked on the black-armored giant atop his camel. As Osi drew close to his target, the Aleke turned to face him, and Osi saw two empty eyes shining out of a Seer's sparkling face. There was nothing human in those eyes—nothing except a hatred as endless as time. Under other conditions, Osi may have halted in fear of what he saw.

But instead, he leapt. He sailed through the air, soaring twice his height, rearing back his sword in both hands. Then he brought the blade down on the small face opening in the Aleke's helm, anticipating the satisfying burst of his enemy's skull.

Instead, the Aleke's moon-blade whistled in an arc and Osi felt a lightning bolt rip through his left arm as everything beneath his elbow was removed in a clean stroke. His forearm continued the momentum of his failed attack, bouncing harmlessly off the Aleke's helm and thudding onto the ground.

There was no pain. Whatever protections the body had against madness must have taken over. He fell to the floor in a daze, waiting to suffer the same fate as Dikende.

But the end didn't come. The Aleke's attention was elsewhere, past Osi, up toward the roof of the Citadel.

There Lumhen stood. Her skin was alive, shining more brilliantly than any of the other Seers Osi had seen, an armor of light. Emanating from her was a churn of power and rage. In her right hand she held her weapon of choice, an iwisa with a long handle ending in a dense, spiked ball.

Lumhen and the Aleke. The City of Truth and the Cult of Tutu. For an infinite moment, the two regarded each other, and the fate of the Forever Desert teetered on the scales of history, ready to crash in either direction.

But the Aleke turned his mount and galloped in the direction from which he'd come. Immediately, the surviving Cultists rushed after him, abandoning their murderous quest.

Then the world was still. None moved. The only sounds were the whispering shift of sand and the gurgled moans of the dying. The Aleke had come and the Aleke had left, and though Osi believed he understood the evil that had visited him that day, he did not truly understand the cruel turn his life had just taken.

4

IN THE AFTERMATH OF what came to be known as the Fall, the City of Truth was numb. More than three hundred had died, yet there were far fewer than three hundred bodies to bury. Most of the slain had been crushed into nothingness by the sand meteor, a phenomenon for which the Peacekeepers had no explanation beyond the old adage.

The Aleke is clever.

Citizens became feral in the face of what they believed was the impending end of civilization. There was mass looting. Businesses burned. Many of those who had been at the Citadel that day died by their own hands, succumbing to the corrosive despair of those who have seen hell but must live as though they haven't.

Stories of what happened that day varied. Some said the Truthseekers had been killed, but that Lumhen had brought Hizojie and Izen back to life. Some said that the Aleke had left as soon as he killed seventy-seven people—a number of sacrifice to the Goddess. Some, sadly, said that Dikende had betrayed the Truthseekers, and that Lumhen had been forced to kill him.

But as varied as the stories were, there was one consistency—a boy. A brave boy who shined like the sun. Who fought like a desert viper. Who had charged the Aleke himself and been his equal.

As numbness threatened to break the city apart, the mysterious boy became the only story that held it together.

All this happened while Osi was at home, in bed, fighting an infection from his severed arm. While stories of his valor spread, he was waking from nightmares covered in sweat, eyes rolling in delirium. As citizens carved statues and wrote songs in his honor, memories of that day were festering in his mind, the past poisoning the present.

It was a week before he was able to sit up without vomiting.

It was a month before he could leave his bed without sobbing in pain.

Once he did, he was surprised by an invitation to the Citadel of Truth. The Peacekeepers took him and his family in a wagon, one pulled by two camels with an interior that was as lush with color and comfort as anything Osi had ever seen. They were fed chunks of fresh fruit and even soft discs of warm bread. As they rode through Central District, scores of citizens lined the streets, jostling to peer through the wagon's windows for a glimpse inside.

The wagon slowed as it arrived at the Citadel, where a crowd waited in the plaza.

Osi felt a sudden seizing of his lungs, a tripling of his heart. It was that day again, the Fall. He already knew what would happen to the people, knew that the meteor would soon descend from the sky and smear them against the newly inlaid stone. It took all his willpower to not shout out in warning, to not jump out of the wagon and run far, far away from the Citadel of Truth.

"It is fine, Osi," said his eldest sister, rubbing his back. She kept her gaze out the window. "You are fine."

Beneath the still-destroyed entrance of the Citadel, the Speaker stood in front of several dozen Peacekeepers in formation. The three surviving Truthseekers were there as well, in rare black robes. They wouldn't be wearing their usual gold on a day like this. Gold was the color of the sun. Of freedom and grandeur and inspiration.

Black was the color of the gods. Of power. Today, they were there as a symbol that the City of Truth was the most powerful city in the Forever Desert and that nothing—not even the Aleke—could change that. A message diminished by the absence of their fourth member.

Osi stepped out of the wagon to the stares of the onlookers. With his family around him, he marched to the front of the assembly, ignoring the eyes on his missing arm.

"Osi, please come forward," the Speaker said.

Osi glanced quickly at his mama, hoping she would walk with him. But all she gave was an encouraging nod, and he continued alone toward the Speaker.

He went down on both knees and saluted, left arm behind his back and right fist going over his heart, then upright against the shoulder.

Except he'd forgotten he was missing his left arm; he felt clumsy, unbalanced.

"Beneath the eyes of the gods," the Speaker said, their voice carrying across the plaza without any aid, "in the words of the Elders, with the mouth of the Speaker: Today, we make a twofold promise. First, a promise of remembrance: to forever honor and remember the Fall. We shall not forget the discord of that day. We shall not forget the subjugation. We shall not forget the injustice. Over three hundred of our citizens were returned to the Goddess. We shall not forget them."

"And they will know peace," the crowd murmured in response.

The Speaker then read the names of the dead, allowing a second of silence after each. By halfway through, Osi's lower back was stiff. By the end, it was screaming in pain. He still didn't understand why his presence was required, but it was too late to question anything. The last name the Speaker read was Dikende the Mighty, and at that, a coldness fell over the plaza.

After a long while, the Speaker took a sip of water and continued.

"And the second promise," they began, with an edge in their voice that made Osi stiffen. If the wise, serene Speaker was angry, then the whole world was about to change. "This is a promise of vengeance. There remain in this world those who seek to end our very existence, and our doctrine of defense will no longer be enough. We must do more than defend. For it has come to pass that the man who orchestrated the Fall, the one known as the Aleke, has stolen our city's sacred God's Eyes."

There was a collective gasp at that, a swell of rage and despair.

The Speaker continued. "The Aleke may sleep well tonight. And tomorrow night. But today I say to you, the Citizens of Truth, that soon will come the day when the Aleke lays down his head to sleep and knows not that he has dreamed his final dream."

"And he will know peace," the crowd responded again, bloodlust on their tongues.

"To my right are your Truthseekers," the Speaker said.

Applause swept through the crowd.

"They saved our city that day," the Speaker continued, "but there was one other who sacrificed himself for our great city."

The sudden feral cries, the absolute howling of grief and pain and encouragement that burst from the crowd sent an icy tremor rippling down Osi's spine. He looked over his shoulder. Every single citizen, young and old, was cheering. Many of them were openly weeping, but that didn't impede their cheers, only made them more desperate. It was as if every emotion they'd felt over the last month was suddenly pouring out of them and into him. He was their avatar, the chosen conduit of their rage and heartbreak, and he was being given their collective strength to accomplish what they individually could not.

"This young man," the Speaker shouted over the crowd's fervor, "is Osi, son of the fallen Senior Peacekeeper Ulodion. He stood beside the Truthseekers against the Aleke and the Cult of Tutu. He thrust his arm into the mouth of evil and flinched not when it bit down upon him. This *boy* . . ."

The Speaker let the word hang, waiting as the crowd's outpouring of emotion ran its course, until there was nothing left of them but the weary husk of hope.

". . . will be the one who fulfills these promises. He is remembrance. He is vengeance. He is, as of this day, our newest Ascendant."

Osi raised his disbelieving face to the Speaker, whose bronze mask revealed nothing.

"Osi, you will have one year," they said. "One year before the Aleke raises his army of Seers. One year to train your body and mind to become a Truthseeker. If you are willing to be our remembrance and vengeance," the Speaker said, "and are willing to slay the Aleke and return the God's Eyes to the City of Truth, please remind us all of the Three Truths."

In the solemn hush of the Citadel's plaza, Osi swept his gaze across the Speaker and the Peacekeepers. He glanced at Clever Hizojie, Izen the Wise, and the Legendary Lumhen, the newest Light of the Truthseekers. He was a one-armed sixteen-year-old who had snuck into a ceremony he wasn't supposed to attend. People often mistook him for a student. His sister had combed his hair for him that morning—not because of his lost arm, but because he did not know how to comb his hair for formal events.

He was the last person the city should rely on.

Just like the Spearman.

Being a hero is not just saving the innocent, it is also punishing the guilty. Baba's words, from years long gone. *Remember the Spearman.*

"The Aleke is cruel," Osi recited, and he felt a reassuring rumble as his city repeated it with him. "The Aleke is clever. The Aleke is coming."

5

THE FIRST MONTH WAS torture. Osi thought his body would grow accustomed to the training, but there was no time for recovery. Each day, the long and grueling exercises whittled him down. He gained a limp from the arduous daily runs, and the skin of his stump reopened from various exercises, forcing him to do even more things with one hand than usual.

While the days sapped his body, the nights sapped his mind. Each night, the Fall replayed itself in his nightmares. Over and over, he watched the Aleke and his Cultists cut down innocent citizens. Except sometimes the citizens were the Truthseekers. Sometimes they were Inusu. Sometimes they were Mama and his sisters, and Osi would have to watch them die a dozen gruesome deaths before he'd wake in a violent sweat.

But consistency makes progress an inevitability. With time and repetition, his muscles tightened, his mind endured, and he found himself feeling like a true Ascendant.

It didn't hurt that Lumhen was his mentor. She was everything he'd imagined her to be, and more. An impetuous leader, a weapons genius, charisma personified. But she also possessed an intensity that Osi hadn't expected, a drive and purpose that left Osi watching with equal parts awe and terror as she pressed impossible weights overhead or hacked so viciously at Izen and Hizojie in sparring that she made splinters of their shields.

Then, she'd transform—from chest heaving and muscles engorged to smiling and sweet, all in an instant.

Three months into his year of training, Osi was finally ready to move beyond just watching the Truthseekers spar.

"Osi the Unfallen," Lumhen called across the training grounds one afternoon, using the nickname that had arisen among the citizens, "train with Izen. Use Sight."

"I . . . do not know how," Osi admitted.

At the Fall, he'd used the power of the God's Eye just from shock. But since then, he'd practiced on his own, with inconsistent results.

Lumhen smiled. "Ah. Izen, teach him."

"Sight is a function of knowledge and conviction," Izen explained. "The scholar Lamizi was the first to articulate a comprehensive—"

"Knowledge is your bow," Lumhen cut in. "The more you have, the stronger your draw. Conviction is your arrow—without it, you are harmless."

Osi closed his eyes and thought of everything he knew. Everything he'd learned from his parents and the Peacekeepers, and his few months with the Truthseekers. And the lessons he'd learned in the Fall. On that knowledge, he rested the arrow of his conviction.

Spearman, guide me.

When he opened his eyes, everything seemed to glow with life. He could See the roughness of the Citadel walls, See the smell of lunch on everyone's breath, See the heat of the clashing of bronze between Hizojie and Lumhen as they began sparring. His skin sparkled with tiny points of light, power given form as calmness and clarity settled into him. With enough conviction, all of the energy around him was his to wield. He just had to know and believe.

Izen thrashed him anyway.

Within minutes, he was exhausted and frustrated and lumped in a dozen places. He resolved to land just one firm strike, something to let him leave the sparring session with some of his dignity intact. He lunged forward, ignoring Izen's painful counterattack, and struck hard— much harder than he'd intended. For a moment, he could See his blunt training spear driving into Izen's abdomen, ramming into her ribs hard enough to bruise them.

Then suddenly, Osi found himself on the ground, his own ribs screaming, the muscles around them hot with damage. He rolled on the floor, clutching his torso and trying to blink the pain away.

"What happened?" he squeezed out.

Lumhen squatted in front of him. "You are fine, Osi," she said, sitting him up and rubbing his chest. "See?"

All of Osi's thoughts disappeared. All he could think about was how close Lumhen's face was to his. How good she smelled. How enveloping her eyes were, consuming him. He stared in silence.

"I did not injure you," Izen said, casually twirling her spear. "That pain is your doing."

"The price of the Seer," Lumhen said, and with a final pat of his chest, she stood. He exhaled a life's worth of tension. "Any pain you cause with your Sight, you yourself will feel."

"But she is fine," Osi asked, nodding at Izen. "Did she not feel it?"

"I did," Izen said. "But not like you."

Lumhen must've seen his confusion. "A Seer's senses are stronger," she explained. "You can see, smell, and hear more than others. And *feel*. But as you learn to control it, that will change."

Osi didn't understand, a position he was more frequently finding himself in.

"So I cannot hit anyone or I will suffer?" he asked. "How can I kill the Aleke if I cannot hurt him?"

"You numb yourself," Hizojie said. He was away from them, sitting with his head leaned back against the lunch table bench, staring at the sky. His voice lacked its usual bite. It was soft and calm, as sincere as Osi had ever heard it. "A Seer does not suffer when he steps on the sand. Because he feels nothing for the sand. That is all people are, Osi. Grains of sand. Burn them, crush them, step on them. You will learn to feel nothing."

Lumhen gave Hizojie an impenetrable look, then she drew her practice iwisa. "Another round," she called out. "Izen, Hizo, together. I will help Osi."

For the rest of the day, Hizojie's words clung to Osi's thoughts. Of the three Truthseekers, he was the one Osi knew least. In the past three months, they had never had a single conversation. Even Izen, who spent most of her days in books, had asked Osi questions about his life—family, interests, experiences. But Hizojie kept his distance.

Hizojie's words never left Osi's mind. They were the first truths Hizojie had ever said to him.

6

THE MONTHS PASSED impatiently, and soon the year was nearing its end. Osi improved in combat just as he had in endurance, and he soon moved on to mastering the Seeing Arts, learning not just to access the power of his God's Eye, but to become fluent in its powers, to enhance his sense of taste during meals, hold whispered conversations from a distance, see subtle differences in behavior and body that could reveal whether someone was lying.

As Osi's Seeing abilities grew, so did his standing among the Truthseekers. Izen taught him to read, and even Hizo warmed to him, often addressing him with the sort of offhand insults he reserved for those close to him. The boy who had idolized the Truthseekers so intensely as a youth became their comrade, joining them for nightly dinners, playing dice games in Izen's chambers, watching holiday parades from the Citadel's ramparts.

In fact, he felt he was more than a comrade. He was a friend.

"We should have left Osi the Unthinking behind," Hizo muttered.

Osi grunted.

It was deep into the night, closer to the sun's rising than its setting. Osi and the Truthseekers were sneaking out of the Citadel to celebrate Lumhen's Known Day, an annual tradition they'd observed since they were Ascendants. It was the only time they were able to enjoy themselves free from the watchful eyes of the Citadel staff and the citizenry.

"He is one of us now, Hizo," Lumhen said. "And I want him here." She tossed a small, secret smile Osi's way.

They traveled through the stately buildings and residences near the Citadel to the festive air of Central District. There, among the elaborate facades that fronted every building and the ambling young people cackling as they strolled, the Truthseekers slipped down a narrow alley and into the basement of a restaurant.

They were greeted by a room lit with lanterns and laughter and warmed by lush carpets from wall to wall. A singer in the center crooned the city's most popular histories, including the story of the Spearman. People sat in small groups around large teapots and hookah pipes, keeping themselves topped off on both as they intently discussed matters important and frivolous alike.

Everyone there knew they were Truthseekers, but they pretended a respectful ignorance, allowing the four to enjoy the night without feeling scrutinized or on duty.

"Who are these people?" Osi asked.

"Izen's inbred cousins," Hizo said, surveying the scene with disgust.

"I studied at the university during our Ascendancy," Izen said. "Many of these are my schoolmates."

Hizo glanced between Izen and some of the others in attendance, struck by the deep resemblance.

"Though some are indeed family," she added.

In Osi's neighborhood, there was a joke that the university was on the edge of the city's Eastern District because when the Aleke attacked, the philosophers would die first. That was about all Osi knew about it. He'd never thought much about academic life or the people who lived it, though he supposed Izen was the sort.

Soon, tea was being poured and hookah coals were being lit, and the winds of conversation carried Osi away. It was just the four of them, and Osi soon came to see the value in being ignored. There was nowhere in the city the Truthseekers could go without being swarmed by admirers. But this space was safe for them, a pocket of the world where the burdens of their role were relieved. Its comfort allowed them to speak about things they couldn't speak about on the training grounds.

"And you, Osi?" Lumhen asked. "What will you do after we defeat the Aleke?"

They'd started with trading theories on what a post-Aleke world would look like, whether there would even be a need for Truthseekers and, if so, how their role might change. Then the question had become more personal, diving into each of their hopes and ambitions. Hizo said he would become a mercenary, tracking down the remaining members of the Cult for a hefty fee. Izen said she would return to her studies.

Osi thought hard, but nothing came to mind. "I . . ." He'd always known the story of his life in a vague way: excel, become a hero, change the world. Only recently had the specific movements of that story become clear: become a Truthseeker, kill the Aleke, bring peace to the city. Yet there was nothing after. Was he supposed to go back and live with Mama and the girls? Rejoin the Peacekeepers? With only one arm, many jobs would be unavailable to him. "I do not know," he finished.

"Osi the Uninteresting," Hizo muttered into his cup. Izen smiled wide—the closest she ever came to laughing.

Lumhen laughed delicately and rolled her eyes. "You have time," she said to Osi. "But you will want to find something. The future must be imagined before it can be made."

Osi chewed on that thought. "What of you, Light Lumhen?" He was never quite sure whether to call her by title, especially in such a casual setting. "What will you do?"

She sighed and looked away for a moment, imagining.

"I will become Speaker," she replied firmly. Her gaze slid from the far side of the room to settle on Osi, and in her eyes he saw the fire of ambition that he admired so much. He understood her; like him, she knew she was destined for great things.

But as far as he knew, the Speaker was chosen by the city's Elders after weeks of nonstop prayer to the Spearman. It was a role assigned for life—not something someone could just choose to be. "How?" Osi asked.

"There are ways," was all Lumhen said. Then she turned her attention back to something on the other side of the room.

"I told you we should have left him," Hizo said. "The boy draws eyes."

* * *

Across the room, seated with their back to the wall, a lone figure had decided not to follow the rule of ignoring the Truthseekers. A head wrap and scarf covered much of their face, but their eyes were visible, dark and curious.

Osi stared back, suspicious.

Lumhen leaned over to him. "You seem to have captured someone's interest."

"I do not see how," he mumbled.

But Lumhen was, of course, correct. The watcher's gaze again and again returned to Osi.

"Go and entertain your fan, Osi the Unremarkable," Hizo said. "Spare us your presence."

Osi shook his head.

"Go on," Lumhen agreed. "Tonight is a rare night. Enjoy it."

The heat in his face was unbearable.

"I am going outside for air," he announced to the amusement of the others.

He left the basement and plunged back into the night, head bowed and body curled against the desert chill. From the alley, he moved into a small roundabout between adjacent buildings, and waited.

It didn't take long.

The stranger entered the courtyard from the same direction Osi had, clad in their head wrap and nervous, inquisitive demeanor. As soon as they saw Osi, they picked up speed, rushing toward him.

Osi's instinct was to use his Sight to defend himself, but he hesitated. He was a Seer now; he had real power, power that could kill someone. It was for use against Cultists, not citizens of the city, even those with ill intent. As they drew closer, he decided to risk hand-to-hand combat, only using his Sight if a weapon appeared.

When he took a fighting stance, they halted their charge.

"Osi," they said. "It is me." They pulled off their head wrap and revealed their full face.

"Inusu . . ." Osi said, stunned.

Then she closed the gap, crossing the courtyard to wrap him in a hug. Osi was too surprised to hug her back.

"Why are you here?" he asked.

"Why are *you* here?" she replied.

For a moment, they were silent, just staring at each other. Then they were taken by laughter until they sat together on the sandy ground.

"How is your arm?" she asked, taking his stump in her hands and inspecting it. "I was worried you would reinfect it."

"I take care of it fine," he lied. "How is your mama? Baba?"

That was followed by a long silence. "You have not been getting my letters," Inusu said. "I thought you were just too busy to respond, but . . . you did not get them."

"Letters?" Osi said.

She had been sending him letters weekly, she explained, little updates about her life and their neighborhood. Her promotion from the Juniors, a birth here, a marriage there.

And other things. How the increased taxes to prepare for the attack on the Aleke were eroding the community, turning comfortable families into struggling ones and struggling ones desperate. How the river had overflowed for the first time in decades, a bad omen. How people were placing all their faith in him to free them from the Aleke's tyranny once and forever.

Osi hadn't heard any of it until that moment. "The letters must be saved for me somewhere."

Inusu bit her lip, eyes wary. "Osi, I wrote other things in my letters too . . . if you are not the one receiving them . . ."

"What?"

She shot to her feet. "It has been too long. If the Truthseekers come looking for us . . ."

"What do you mean?"

"They are not what they appear to be, Osi. I have met people from—"

"Osi?"

Lumhen's voice carried across the courtyard, leading the three Truthseekers out of the narrow alley, shadows in the moonlight.

Inusu reached behind her back. Osi climbed to his feet.

"It is me," he said.

"And who is this?" Lumhen asked.

They stood in a row, casual. But Osi had been with them long enough to know what it felt like when they were preparing for battle.

"It is fine," he said, extending a pacifying hand. "This is my friend, In—"

"Osi the Unfallen flatters me," Inusu said in a strange, husky voice. She lowered to her knees and dropped her gaze to the earth. "I am no friend. Just a citizen, and a great admirer of his. Of you all."

Osi frowned but didn't speak.

Nor did anyone else. Silence.

"It is late," Hizo finally said. "We should all go. Lumhen?"

Lumhen stood still for a second, then strode across the courtyard, stopping right in front of Inusu. She reached out and lifted Inusu from her kneeling position, looking into her eyes with all the gentle regality Osi admired her for.

"Every citizen is a friend of the Truthseekers," she said, patting Inusu on both shoulders. "It was Inusu, eh?"

Osi had known Inusu all his life. He knew what her different expressions meant. And hours later, when he was back in his bed in the Citadel, unable to sleep due to the tempest in his mind, he couldn't stop thinking about how calmly blank her eyes had been, how measured and even her breathing was.

"Be well," Lumhen had said before she led them out of the courtyard, where Inusu had remained. Terrified.

7

OSI NEVER FOUND Inusu's letters. His chamber servant told him there were no held messages for him, and when Osi visited the Citadel postmaster on his own, he was told the same. He didn't feel any need to read them—Inusu had updated him on everything important—but he was surprised that a place as orderly as the Citadel couldn't find them. He wrote a letter to Inusu explaining the situation, but then his mind turned to the impending mission against the Aleke.

He never noticed that he didn't get a reply.

Then it was time for his Ascendance. He stood before his room's mirror, clad in a simple red agbada. The Citadel tailor had sewn it with asymmetrical sleeves to better accent his missing arm. It was a fashion he'd taken to in the last few months, and he'd heard some of the civilians were taking after him, slashing their left sleeves short.

His missing arm still itched sometimes. Worse, there were nights when it was filled with pain, like a knifepoint excavating his flesh. Sometimes, he would react to the pain with joy, thinking that somehow his limb had grown back. But when he looked down, he realized it was just his body lying to him the way the desert does, a mirage of how he used to be. A reminder of what he'd sacrificed, no matter how foolishly, to become the man he was.

"Ascendant Osi," a chambermaid sang through the door. "Are you ready?"

Head high, shoulders back, every inch the Truthseeker he finally felt himself to be, Osi went out into the hall. Citadel staff lined both sides, and as he strode past them, they smiled in pride, some whispering words of encouragement and praise. For a year, they had clothed him, cleaned after him, kept him fed. He owed them a debt that he was determined to repay.

He soon reached the top of the Citadel. There, his comrades

were waiting in Truthseeker gold: Izen the Wise, Clever Hizojie, the Legendary Lumhen. They crossed the roof, over to the great golden doors. The Temple of Ayé, he was told it was called. The only remaining temple to an old and forgotten god. Up close, Osi could see stories from all across history etched into it. All that history fought for, bled for, died for. A fight he would soon take up.

The doors groaned open, revealing a tall but narrow hall with smooth marble forming the walls and floor. As the Light of the Truthseekers, Lumhen led the way, Hizo and Izen side by side behind her. Osi was last, head bowed as instructed, an image of humility.

The Speaker's room was at the end of the hall, unremarkable but for the rows and rows of portraits along the back wall. There were almost two dozen men and women painted in stunning detail, as if the artist had stolen their faces and pinned them onto canvas. The last portrait was of a man in his middle years, with heavy brows, sunken, marred cheeks, and a forehead elongated by a receding hairline. His face was stern, but his eyes were wise, deep, full of emotion.

The Speaker stood right beside the final portrait, their pale brown eyes staring out from behind the bronze mask, etched with a face that was part human, part reptile.

Osi knelt, head bowed.

"Beneath the eyes of the gods," the Speaker said, "in the words of the Elders, with the mouth of the Speaker: Today, we gather for the Ascendance of Osi, son of Senior Peacekeeper Ulodion. A year ago this day, he was recognized as an Ascendant of the City of Truth. Today, he seeks to be recognized as a Truthseeker. He was raised to Ascendant by the city, but a Truthseeker must be accepted by Truthseekers. Who among you will stand for him?"

"I, Lumhen, daughter of Onenki, Light of the Truthseekers, will stand for Osi," Lumhen said, rising to her feet.

"I, Izen, daughter of Azen, will stand for Osi," Izen said quickly, as if she were ready to move on to another topic. She stood.

Silence. Osi kept his gaze on the ground, confused.

"Clever Hizojie," the Speaker asked in a near whisper. "Do you stand?"

Osi couldn't help looking over at Hizo—the man hadn't moved. He remained on his knees, head bowed.

"I . . ." Hizo began, uncharacteristically solemn. "I, Hizojie, an unclaimed child, stand for Osi."

He rose.

Osi exhaled.

The Speaker finished the ceremony with a private prayer for Osi, that he would fight bravely and, should he fall, be remembered truly. Then they went outside to the reconstructed edge of the Citadel terrace. A year prior, Osi had stood on that very edge with these same Truthseekers, watching the Aleke's massacre unfold.

Now, he looked down on the fevered populace of the City of Truth, a crush of thousands peering up at him from the plaza below.

The sight reminded him of a moment from boyhood. After his baba died, Osi had taken to wearing one of his Peacekeeper uniforms around the city, despite its overlarge fit. One day, one of the neighborhood children had said Osi would never be a Peacekeeper like his baba, not out of malice but in the honest manner that children speak, using words and watching to see their effect. Osi hadn't responded, not because he decided to be the more reasonable party but because for a slice of a moment, he believed that what the child said was true.

Since then, his life had been a series of such events, people who purported to know what heights he was and wasn't allowed to rise to. Teachers, mentors, his own family—all had believed in only the smallest version of him. He'd never forgiven himself for believing that child, even for a second.

Below him, the citizenry was openly weeping, screaming in pain, self-flagellating with three-pronged whips. It was an Ascendance unlike any other. For a year, they had maintained their hope and patience, but that was now at an end. They wanted vengeance. And they were entrusting Osi to fulfill it. The whole city believed in him, finally, the way he had always believed in himself.

Osi snapped down into a bow, face toward the floor so no one could see him crying.

But the Speaker and the Truthseekers remained upright, watching each other in silent agreement that their plan was to move forward.

That Osi's life would soon come to an end.

8

CLAD IN TRUTHSEEKER GOLD, Osi stood in the wagon's front seat, wind whipping at his robes as he admired the empty stretch of rolling dunes around him. He'd insisted on sitting in the front, beside Izen. He wanted to see his first mission unfold before his eyes. To witness the crossing of the land between the city and the Cult, feel its disquieting emptiness. Every Truthseeker who had ever lived had made the two-day journey, and now Osi shared that experience.

He didn't know the world could be so silent. There was no children's laughter, no parents arguing, no greatmamas and greatbabas cackling out in front of their homes. It had been hours since they'd heard the last birdcall—birds saw no need to be this far into the Forever Desert. The only sound was the wind, but even that sounded different. Osi had always known wind to be a pinched shriek. Here, the wind had the voice of an elder: deep and wide, pushing on him like a current.

They traveled at dusk to avoid the sun's heat, driving their camels without respite to escape the claws and fangs of nocturnal predators. The desert was blue beneath the moonlight, the swirls and stars of the heavens a painted canvas above them. Off to their left and right, small flecks of white glittered out of the sand. They were rare at first, but as they traveled farther into the desert, the white bits came to mirror the stars above.

"Why is this sand so white?" Osi asked Izen.

"Oh." She looked around like she hadn't noticed. "Yes. It is bone."

Bones? Osi didn't understand. "How? They are too small to be bones," he said.

"I did not say bones. *Bone.* The dust of three centuries of war. When civilians fight, bones are broken. When Seers fight, bones explode."

Osi swallowed, suddenly hesitant to breathe too deeply. They were traveling through an open graveyard.

"Are you afraid?" Izen asked.

"No," he lied.

As day began to break, they parked the wagon and climbed into its cabin, a great clay barrel laid horizontally that could easily fit ten. Inside, they had all the food, clothes, and weapons they needed for the mission. They ate quickly, then went over the mission before sleeping in shifts.

Osi and Izen shared a watch. Osi had hoped to spend more time with Lumhen, but Izen was good company too. He'd come to appreciate her toneless, clinical style of speech and unintentional humor. She was largely quiet, though, which left Osi sitting on the lip of the wagon as the sun beat hot overhead, thinking about what the next day would bring. It had been a year since he'd seen the Aleke in the flesh, but Osi saw him nearly every night in his nightmares. He wondered whether a year was enough to truly prepare for such a fight. Dikende had trained his whole life and still fell. And maybe the Aleke wasn't alone. He may have already doled out the God's Eyes to his most barbaric soldiers, and the Truthseekers were walking into a fight against an army of Seers.

Do not just fear that you may do wrong. Fear that you may not do right.

In the lonely quiet of the Forever Desert, his baba's words brought him some comfort.

When the sun began to bleed into the horizon again and they resumed traveling, it wasn't long before Osi began to see shapes in the distance. It was full night by the time they were close enough to see the details of those shapes, though Osi wasn't sure if he was seeing correctly.

"Is that it?" he asked, incredulous.

Ahead of them were ramshackle slums, two- and three-story brick structures in varying states of decay and collapse. Laundry was strung between buildings like spider silk, dangling above empty lots filled with refuse. Here and there, balls of lamplight illuminated one hunched shadow or another, revealing the shapes of Cultists scuttling beneath their low, crumbling ceilings.

Osi had never seen such destitution, not even in the city's Sunrise District. This was supposed to be the Forever Desert, the endless empire of the immortal Aleke and his Cult of Tutu, against whom all of the battles in history had been fought. The fear they'd lived under, the siege they'd suffered . . . *this* was their enemy?

"It is beautiful," Izen said, slowing the wagon to a halt.

"Eh?" Osi couldn't imagine anything less beautiful. The place smelled atrocious just from looking at it.

"City life is restricted by duty," she said. "To the people, to the Speaker. Here, there is only the mission. It is my belief that this is how life should be: no rules, no responsibilities, nothing to submit to but our own desires. We can do whatever we wish."

As Izen looked upon the Aleke's territory, moonlight shining in her eyes, there was something in her demeanor and in the uncharacteristic excitement in her voice that Osi found unsettling.

A feeling that had come far too late.

"Truthseekers, with me," Lumhen said, hopping out of the cabin, Hizo behind her. "From here we go on foot."

9

THE STREETS WERE DUSTY. The air was dry and bore a stench of piss and feces. There were no forts. No watchtowers. Not even reinforced doors. In the distance loomed the Aleke's Sacrificial Tower. It was said to be the Aleke's home, from which he hung the children of insurrectionists as a warning to others who might dare to revolt. Massive as it was, it was built of shoddy, brittle brick, no comparison at all to the Citadel of Truth.

As the Truthseekers crept along the empty late-night streets of the Aleke's territory, Osi struggled to understand the poverty and squalor he was seeing. The Peacekeepers numbered nearly two thousand strong at full health. Even against iron weapons, the forces of the City of Truth should have been more than capable of overrunning these slums.

How is this our enemy?

Izen's informants had told her of an abandoned house near the Sacrificial Tower that would serve as base of operations for the assault and a retreat point for the aftermath. She led them down a narrow alley and into a squat home made of iron sheeting that was so filthy and foul-smelling it made Osi's eyes water.

"Good choice, Izen," Hizo said. "We will distract the Aleke by smelling like shit."

"It is the only iron building nearby," she countered. "Therefore, our use of Sight will not draw attention. The smell, though unpleasant, is not fatal."

"Only if I do not kill myself," Hizo muttered.

Once Izen's informants confirmed the Aleke's whereabouts, the mission would begin. But until then, they waited, laying down on sleeping mats, sharpening their weapons, praying.

For the Truthseekers, this was routine. They had performed dozens of missions in the Forever Desert, even during their years as Ascendants.

Osi found himself unable to calm his mind or even slow his breathing. On every side were enemies. Cultists. People sworn to madness and murder. Any noise could bring a swarm descending upon them, iron blades plunging in and out of his chest. The Aleke could be outside their door at that very moment, breath rattling in his black armor.

Everyone in the City of Truth lived in fear of the Aleke. But there was a difference, Osi now understood, between living in fear of an oppressor from a distance and living in the oppressor's shadow.

A sound at the door sent Osi's blood pounding through his veins. He was on his feet, short spear in hand, eyes wide and locked on the entrance. The other Truthseekers flared with light.

"Izen," Lumhen whispered, so low that only a Seer would be able to hear it. "Are they yours?"

Hizo moved without sound, approaching the door as a muffled voice issued from the other side. He had his dagger in hand and held position just beside the opening, his entire body slack, the prospect of violence seeming to calm him.

"Osi," Lumhen whispered, and he turned in her direction. She was flat against the far wall, her skin dulled, hiding in the darkness. She nodded her head, signaling for him to move. He rushed to stand between her and Izen.

The door opened slowly, iron creaking on its rusted hinges. A head poked in, that of a man in his middle years with a gaunt face in mismatching hues.

He disappeared back outside, then reappeared with two children ahead of him, one perhaps approaching teenage years and the other a half dozen years younger.

They took a few steps before the youngest looked directly at Osi. Her eyes must have been still adjusting to the darkness. She slowed, peering at him uncertainly for a moment until she realized what she was seeing. Then her mouth yawned open and there was an intake of breath, but before any sound could be issued, Hizo's hand clamped tight on her face, smothering her scream.

The sequence repeated itself again with the man, but Hizo did not have another free hand. He slid the dagger into the side of the man's neck and slashed forward, expelling his throat from his body. The man crumpled in a gurgle.

Then there was the teenager.

"Stop!" Osi hissed, hand out in front of him to get everyone's attention. "Stop! Hizo, please!"

He wasn't certain he was even speaking to Hizo. He was just speaking to the world, to the sequence of events playing out before him—he needed it all to stop. Over the course of a year, he'd prepared himself to kill the Aleke and his Cultists. But not this.

"They are innocent," Osi promised. "He will not scream. He will not scream."

Spearman, protect us. Spearman, guide us. Spearman, protect us. Spearman, guide us.

Thankfully, the boy didn't scream. All he did was stare at the man's unmoving body.

Hizo paused, then looked over at Lumhen.

"Osi, you know what we are here to do," Lumhen said. "We cannot afford a mistake."

"There is no mistake," he assured, breathless. "Please."

"Baba . . ." the little girl cried, muffled by Hizo's hand.

In that moment, it all came together. A baba, destitute and unable to provide, found shelter in an abandoned home. Even its filth and stench were preferable to whatever situation they'd escaped from.

So he'd thought.

"Lumhen, please," Osi begged.

Lumhen heard him.

But she did not listen.

"Hizo," she said, and added a firm, commanding nod.

* * *

Spearman, forgive us.

They stacked the bodies in the far corner, a blanket tossed over them. Osi sat on the floor, knees up against his chest. He tried to rub his tired eyes, but his hand was shaking too much.

"Sleep, Osi." Lumhen's voice. "Izen will tell us when to be ready."

All his life, Osi had imagined his baba had died honorably, just like in the stories. Overcoming impossible odds to reach his final foe, only to fall nobly, valiantly, to an opponent whose evil would have to be defeated by another.

But Osi knew death now. He'd seen it at the Fall and again here. There was no story to it. No romance. No final battle against an equal foe. Only the crushed skull, gashed throat, and split torso of a person defeated by a power greater than them.

How could he ever sleep again?

"What did we do?" he asked himself.

"They were Cultists," Lumhen said. "Better them than us."

Osi shook his head. The little one had spoken. "They were not Cultists. They had tongues."

"They all have tongues, Osi," Izen said absently, looking out between a space in the walls of the shack. "The incorrect notion that the Cultists are untongued derives from—"

"It is only a story," Lumhen interrupted.

"But they looked like us," he said, and immediately realized what a fool he sounded.

The Cultists from the Fall had been soldiers in their prime—lean, feral, full of hatred. These Cultists had been a family. There was no hatred in them, just fear. Osi had only seen fear like that one other time—the Fall. He'd seen it in the other Juniors. In all the Peacekeepers whose lives had been stolen by the Cultists. In Hizo and Izen as they watched Dikende's brains be dashed across the plaza. In himself.

He'd never imagined that he would one day be the cause of such fear.

"Osi—" Lumhen began, but Hizo, leaning calmly against a wall, cut her off.

"Have I gone mad?" Hizo asked. "Why are we consoling him?"

"Hizo . . ." Lumhen warned.

"Save your anger, my Light," Hizo shot back, returning his gaze to Osi. "Did I not tell you? Numb yourself. A whole year and you learned *nothing*."

His voice echoed off the iron, filling the room.

Hizo exhaled frustration. "Osi the Unfit is not ready for combat. We will reclaim him when we are finished."

"Osi is a Truthseeker," Lumhen countered. "He comes with us."

For a blink, Hizo's expression changed. From rage to pleading. From disgust to desperation.

Osi looked between the two, sensing that there was something more to their disagreement, but not understanding what was really at stake.

"It is time," Izen said, turning away from her vantage point.

Lumhen reiterated that they were undertaking an assassination mission, not a combat one. Eliminate the Aleke, recover the God's Eyes, and retreat. If all went well, they would be on their way home by morning.

"One way or another," she said, eyeing each of them, "this is where it ends."

Had Osi known what she truly meant, he would have fled right then, deep into the Forever Desert, as far away from the Truthseekers as he could run.

10

SPEARMAN, PROTECT ME, Osi prayed for the hundredth time as he crouched against the wall of the Aleke's safe house. Unlike the narrow iron shacks in the slums, this was a sturdy, tan-brick structure, surrounded by desert as far as could be seen. There were no exterior guards, of course—any sign of armed men in broad daylight would've revealed that someone important was inside. The only way to know whether there were guards was with Sight.

"For truth," Lumhen said. After a moment, her skin erupted with overlapping rings of light.

A scalding wind of emotion swept over Osi. He wanted to weep until he was as dry as the desert. He wanted to flee, screaming like a madman back across the Silence. Pain flared in his stump, tears stung his eyes. He was afraid of the Forever Desert, of the Aleke, and after the night prior, he was beginning to fear the Truthseekers. He wanted his mama and his sisters, Inusu, and his old life as a Junior.

It was a familiar foe, this fear. And to his misfortune, he defeated it as he always had.

Do not fear that you may do wrong. Fear that you may not do right.

He had journeyed too far to turn back. He took a calming breath and used his own Sight, allowing him to See a huddle of people in the building, one of them glowing with the unmistakably thick presence of a Seer.

That would be him.

The Aleke.

In his year of training, Osi had learned that the lethality of the Truthseekers came not from how much individual power they held, but from how they used it. Rather than turning it on their enemies, they turned it first on each other, absorbing and amassing what was given to them, passing it from comrade to comrade until the final Truthseeker unleashed it all on a target like the tip of a cracked whip.

Once Izen's hand came down on his back, his training took over. He absorbed the energy and passed it with a punch to Hizo's shoulder, who smacked the flat of his curled blade against the back of Lumhen's head, whose shoulder charge blasted the brick door into shrapnel.

Hizo was first into the breach, Osi and Izen following behind. There were six enemies inside, five of whom appeared to be regular people—thin and dirty and so possessed by terror at the presence of the Truthseekers that Osi could smell it radiating from them.

The sixth, the Aleke, was impassive. He stared back from within the shelter of his full suit of black hippo armor and his eyes were devoid of fear. Devoid of any emotion at all.

This was supposed to be a surprise attack. Why was the Aleke in full armor?

Then came Lumhen. As she flashed past them into the room they all struck her, passing all the energy they could into their Light. She shined brilliantly from a million dots of iridescence, her power so thick she seemed coated in sunlight. She launched herself, the floor beneath her feet cratering from the force, her eyes glowing with a godless wrath, iwisa reared back over her head and arcing down with all the weight and certainty of death.

When Lumhen's iwisa met the Aleke's scythe, a swell of energy blasted outward. The two Cultists nearest the impact were flattened from the force, belly pressed to back, innards crushed out through every available orifice in a cloud of red smoke. The other three Cultists were thrown into and through the building's brick walls, emerging as mangles of splintered bones. Izen stretched out her arms, absorbing and redirecting the force of the blast away from Osi and Hizo.

Once Lumhen landed, she attacked in full. All the hours of watching her spar hadn't prepared Osi for what she was capable of. In training, she was powerful but patient. Destructive but restrained.

Here, she was a maelstrom of violence. The air around her shimmered like desert heat. Between bone-shattering bashes from her spiked iwisa, sand swirled up from the ground beside her, lashing at the Aleke's armor and leaving sharp grooves in the hippo hide. She was what Osi was supposed to be—the city's vengeance. He could feel three centuries of rage in each burst of weapon against weapon, in each stabbing jut of sand; he could hear the pained howl in each whistled arc.

Even then, the Aleke managed to drive her back with a roaring sweep of his scythe, bringing a pause to the battle.

The plan had been to have Lumhen cave in the Aleke's head before he even knew they had breached the building. But the Aleke had been prepared. He was armed and armored, and now that Osi could reflect on the scene, he realized that the Cultists who had been in the room were too frail, young, and wide-eyed at the appearance of Truthseekers to be the Aleke's top advisers. They must have been just ordinary citizens, or even prisoners, sacrificed to trick the Truthseekers.

The Aleke is cruel.

Something was wrong.

Izen saw it first. "Lumhen . . ." she said.

As the dust of battle settled, Osi looked around. Where parts of the wall had been blown out, he could see Cultists in the distance. Not the frail civilians that had been blown to bits in Lumhen's initial attack, but the ones from the Fall. Armored, pale iron blades in their hands, bodies hard and eyes dead.

All around the Truthseekers, hundreds of Cultists converged on the safe house. They were surrounded.

Then there was a sound like stones falling into a dry well. A sinking rhythm, cold and raspy and mirthless.

The Aleke was laughing.

*   *   *

The Aleke is clever.

It was the same as the Fall. The Aleke wasn't simply stronger, he was smarter. He somehow knew everything the Truthseekers would do before they did it and had perfect counters for their strategies.

In seconds, the Cultists would converge on the building. In close quarters, the skill of the Truthseekers was unparalleled. Every drop of blood the Cultists drew would cost them dozens of lives. Against a normal foe, the Truthseekers could stay and fight, and even win.

But the Aleke was no normal foe. He wouldn't hesitate to sacrifice wave after wave of Cultists if that was what it took to defeat the Truthseekers.

"Retreat," Lumhen said through clenched teeth. "With me."

She drew back her iwisa and slammed it into the wall beside her.

The impact shockwaved through the building, collapsing the entire wall and bringing the ceiling down on top of them. Izen was there again, absorbing the energy of the falling bricks and using it to blast rubble away, opening a path out of the building and into the desert.

Lumhen led the charge, running directly at the approaching Cultists. Osi felt outside himself, watching his body follow her, doing as it was trained to do while his mind told him to turn around and fight. He'd already sacrificed his arm in the fight with the Aleke. Let this be the end, even if it meant death. Stay and fight and finish it once and for all.

"To the cliff!" Lumhen shouted, pointing past the Cultists to a short cliff that led back toward the slums. It was at least five strides high, not an unreasonable jump for a Seer, but too high for the Cultists to pursue.

But first they had to get there, and the Cultists had iron.

It made no difference. Lumhen's iwisa churned through them, batting limbs across the sand, caving heads, creating a space in which anything that dared enter, died.

They punched through the Cultists' line and sped on to the base of the cliff, where they all leapt up, easily reaching the edge. But Osi fell short, catching it only by his fingertips. Izen appeared over him, but she did not bend down to help.

"You were a more than adequate companion, Osi."

"Yes, thank you, help me up!"

Lumhen appeared then. Hizo was just behind her, but he was looking away at nothing, his face contorted in anguish.

Lumhen smiled, warm and dimpled. "It is a necessary sacrifice, Osi," she said. "You understand?"

She kicked him so hard his eardrum burst. His Sight evaporated. He plummeted, dropping for an eternity before he crashed back to the sand, his knee cracking and buckling upon impact.

He was too confused for heartbreak. Too stunned to feel betrayed. He revisited memories in the way of a rejected lover, searching in vain for the moment that would explain everything, not realizing that moment had occurred in the heart, a place he couldn't see.

With more time, the pain of abandonment would likely have consumed him. But the Cultists were upon him immediately, dozens of them circling him at the base of the cliff like scavengers. Then there was that sound, the dry well, the rasping rhythm. The Aleke emerged from among his Cultists, taking a position in front of them.

He was laughing again.

Osi climbed up on his one good leg, hefting his short spear, raising his shield. In the end, he supposed none of it mattered. Baba had died a Peacekeeper. Osi would die a Truthseeker. Maybe his sisters would have children, and one of them would hear their uncle's story and take up the fight against the Aleke. Maybe, a dozen generations in the future, Osi's line would be the one to end the siege, free the city, change the world.

Osi raised his shield as the Aleke's scythe whistled down onto him. He took the blow, but the shield bashed back into his face, exploding his teeth.

He stabbed his spear up into the Aleke's helm, hoping beyond reason that the Aleke would be slow, careless, overconfident. Instead, the scythe's blunt end parried his strike, the force snapping his wrist and sending his weapon spinning across the sand.

He let out an incoherent roar, blood spraying from his broken mouth, tears leaking from his broken heart, unarmed and beyond the limits of his rational mind.

In response, the Aleke drove an armored fist into Osi's throat with a hollow crunch. The world blinked, and he found himself looking up at the sky.

His journey had started this way, he remembered: staring up at the sky and struggling to breathe around the God's Eye in his throat. Maybe that had been an omen. Or maybe it was the natural course of life—from a helpless beginning to a helpless end.

The Aleke entered his vision, a black giant against a blue sky.

Osi thought about his sisters and Mama, Inusu and the Peacekeepers. And even though he tried not to, he thought about Izen, about Hizo, about Lumhen. Lumhen, most of all.

He wanted to live.

Spearman, protect me, he prayed. It was a modest prayer. No longer to become a hero, just to live another day. It was a fair ask, he thought.

But the Aleke's final strike whipped down and removed any further thoughts from Osi's mind.

PART II

11

A NECESSARY SACRIFICE.

Osi dangled, suspended in midair. He couldn't open his eyes. There was too much pain. Throat, pain. Knee, pain. Pain in the raw spaces of his mouth where teeth were missing. Pain in the stump where his arm used to be.

The pain of betrayal had finally arrived as well. A new pain. All the shared runs and workouts, all the hours of sparring. The meals and games and conversations. All those times he'd made a mistake and Lumhen had given him a small smile or a light hand on his shoulder, reassuring him that she understood and that she was there for him even when he failed himself. Each time he reached for a happy memory, the pain was there, reminding him that the happiness was a lie. It was a pain that transcended time, seeping into the past, staining painless moments painful.

Why? he thought.

Osi could do nothing but investigate his memories of the past year, swinging from anger to tears, blaming everyone and himself in equal doses. Nothing he found brought him any closer to answering the question in any of its forms.

Why did Lumhen kick me?

Why was I ever chosen in the first place?

Why did I not know this was coming?

Why am I still alive?

Time passed at its own discretion. When the pain in his eyes diminished, he was able to take in his surroundings. He was in an iron box of a room, cramped and musty, with a thin sheet metal door. Blood was strewn across nearly every surface, even the ceiling, its stench sharp in his nose. His arms were suspended from the ceiling by chains, the shackles around his right wrist and his left stump biting into his skin.

As he was trying to adjust his arms into a less painful position, the door opened.

The man that entered was old, shrunken by time until he was not much larger than Osi's mama. But he was still leanly muscled, his veins visible even in the dim candlelight. He had deeply sunken and puckered cheeks, and his bald head and beardless face were a stark contrast to the pair of bushy eyebrows that dominated the space above his eyes.

Osi recognized him immediately. Though he didn't know why or from where.

"Osi, son of Ulodion, Truthseeker of the City of Lies," the old man said in a calm rasp as he closed the door behind himself. The City of Lies—a name that few would dare utter, yet this man used it so casually. "Before you make any movements, allow me to warn you of the consequences of any action." His smile was genuine but restrained.

Osi couldn't have moved even if he wanted to.

"Good," he said. He produced a pale leather pouch from his khaftan pocket, dipped his hand into it, and pulled out a palm full of roasted peanuts. Then he sat cross-legged on the ground and tossed a peanut into his mouth, chewing as he spoke. "I am Obasa, and I am the minister of interrogation for what you call the Cult of Tutu. You are free to leave at any moment; even with iron, it is impossible to truly cage a man whose power is the world itself. However . . ." He looked up, and Osi's eyes followed. Above them, the chains around Osi's arms met and merged before disappearing into a hole in the ceiling. "We are in a tower. Those chains around you go outside this tower, where they wrap around a little boy. He is years younger than you, and smaller as well. But his chains are not around his wrists, like yours. They are around his neck. And each step you take forward toward this door will tighten and tighten and tighten the chain around that boy's neck until his head will—*gbo!*—right off his shoulders. Of course, I would never underestimate a Truthseeker. If, perhaps, you find a way to break those chains, then Tower Boy will fall to his death. I do not know much about you, Osi, but you do not seem a man who kills innocents."

The matter-of-fact tone; the gentle facial expressions and warm, soft voice; the way he only made eye contact at the end of sentences—

Osi hated everything about this Obasa. But he was right. Osi wasn't willing to kill an innocent. Enough innocents had died.

A *necessary sacrifice.*

But Osi was learning that no one could be trusted.

He summoned his strength for a trickle of Sight, just enough to check if there was truly a boy chained outside. He was able to See some form of life, dozens of strides above the ground. Obasa wasn't lying about this, at least.

"You see the dilemma, eh?" Obasa continued. "But you will learn I am a kind old man, Osi. So I have provided for you another way. A simple way."

He was enjoying this. The twinkle in his eye said as much. He tossed more peanuts into his mouth, waiting for Osi to speak before continuing.

Osi's throat was still crushed from what the Aleke had done to him. Even speaking a few words strained him enough to make him sweat.

"What is it?" he forced himself to ask with just the crumbs of his voice. He had no plan to escape—he didn't know where he would go even if he somehow managed to. But he at least wanted to get out of the shackles.

"I will ask you a question," Obasa said. "There is neither a right nor wrong answer. There is only honesty and deceit. If you answer with honesty, I will have my soldiers remove your chains. You will be free to leave."

Osi stared hard at the man, then gave a slow nod.

"Why are you here?" Obasa asked.

The pain of failure and betrayal filled him.

"To kill the Aleke," he rasped.

Obasa stood, left the room, and locked the door behind him.

*   *   *

There was no sun to watch rise. No moon to track through its phases. Just the same thin door, the same iron prison spattered in old, black blood. Osi lost all feeling in his arms. He was given food and water, but only enough to survive, which had the bittersweet benefit of limiting how often he soiled himself. He did not know how many days had passed, but he had fallen asleep five times.

Each time he woke, Obasa was there.

"Why are you here?"

"To kill the Aleke."

"Why are you here?"

"To kill the Aleke."

"Why are you here?"

"To kill the Aleke."

"Why are you here?"

"To kill the Aleke."

The fifth time, he tried something else.

"Why are you here?"

"To take back the city's God's Eyes."

The first four times, Obasa had simply risen and left. This time, he laughed first.

Osi knew that torture wasn't supposed to make sense. It added to the feeling of helplessness, made the victim feel as if the enemy was unpredictable.

And despite himself, Osi knew it was working.

"They must think you are dead," Osi said to himself in the lonely cell. Even with no nourishment, his body was healing, the gift of a swallowed God's Eye. So he sometimes spoke aloud to test his throat's recovery. And to hear his own voice, to remind himself he was still a person. "Mama and the girls . . ."

So many years ago, during an attack on the city's outskirts, his baba had left home and never returned—another fallen Peacekeeper in an endless war. That day had changed Osi. He would never forget how much he and his mama and his sisters had cried when a young Peacekeeper arrived at their home to deliver the news.

They were going to suffer it all over again. Another restless man, rushing into the desert to die.

You think you are always right, Osi. One day you will learn you are a fool like everyone else, and that you should have listened to your betters.

His mama was right.

A necessary sacrifice.

"What is wrong with me?"

Osi remembered sobbing, but he didn't remember falling asleep. When he woke, as always, Obasa was waiting.

"Good morning, Osi," he said, cross-legged with his back against the door, nibbling from his pouch of roasted peanuts. "You grow tired, eh? There is no shame in it. Even a Truthseeker tires."

"Please," Osi said, and he cursed his cowardice as the word left his lips. But he was scared. Scared to die, scared to live, scared he would twitch in his sleep and kill the child outside the tower. He just wanted it to end. "I have told you why I am here."

"You have," Obasa agreed, "but only with lies."

"I do not know what you want."

The man smiled his usual tight smile. "You are much like my greatson. He is a soldier too, though I did not desire that path for him. But he is stubborn. And determined. The sort of boy who would rather lose an arm than confess his wrongness." His eyes traced Osi's stump.

"Please."

"Why are you here?"

"To . . . I . . . To kill the Aleke, please . . ."

He was still begging his throat raw when Obasa shut the cell door behind him.

"Good morning, Osi."

Through tired, puffed eyes, Osi awoke to see Obasa sitting on the floor, peanuts in hand.

"Why are you here?"

If Osi did nothing, he would eventually die, and the child would live. If he summoned his energy and brought the tower crashing down on Obasa's bald head, he might live, and the child would die. He had the power to do it. Maybe that was how this had to end, with another necessary sacrifice.

Being a hero is not just saving the innocent, it is also punishing the guilty.

But what if there was no way to punish the guilty without also punishing the innocent?

Do not fear that you may do wrong. Fear that you may not do right.

Another useless wisdom; he no longer knew what was right and what was wrong.

Remember the Spearman.

They were the only words of Baba's that still made sense—where the innocent were guilty and the guilty innocent; where right was wrong and wrong was right. The Spearman, at least, was still true.

Yet Osi had prayed and prayed and prayed for the Spearman to be his guide. And where had it brought him?

"Why are you here?"

He had really believed that becoming a Truthseeker was the destiny for which he'd been born. He'd really believed that Lumhen was his friend. Maybe more.

He no longer knew what to believe.

"I came seeking truth," he sighed.

"Good," Obasa said.

Osi raised his head as Obasa climbed to his feet, dusting his hands against each other.

"You answered honestly," the old man said. "You are free to leave. But first . . ." Obasa's skin became light, bathing the room in luminescence. Discs of iridescence overlapped across his body, each the size of a man's hand and just as thick. Osi knew it was Sight, but Obasa's power resembled other Seers the way a song resembles a scream. *This* was what a Seer was supposed to look like. Not with sparkling pores like some hero in a romance story, but with skin like the scales of some divine beast, armored in sun, burning shadows into mist. ". . . allow me to give you what you seek," Obasa said.

12

WHEN OBASA LAID HIS hand on Osi's head, Osi's mind went black. Black, the presence of all color; and so the void of Osi's mind was the presence of all time, an infinite overlapping of knowledge and reality. Then Osi could feel Obasa's presence, siphoning away layer after layer of the blackness until an image began to emerge, bright with color.

Osi looked down on a city in ruin. The desert seemed to be consuming civilization, with tin shack homes built among rampant dunes, no clear delineation between city streets and the wilds of nature. There wasn't a tree in sight, not a single leaf, not a drop of water. It was uninhabitable.

Yet here people lived. Osi stood among them as they trudged about their days. Children, their legs as thin and brittle as dying branches, marched to school. Adults whose rib cages pressed against the thin fabric of their clothes dragged themselves round and round down the tiered pits of iron quarries.

These people were barely surviving.

And yet.

In the distance, a structure dominated the horizon. High on a rocky plateau, it was a towering palace, reminiscent of the Citadel of Truth, but brown brick rather than gray stone, pointed rather than squared, and draped in resplendence—with swirls of colorful gems inlaid along its base—rather than stripped down in martial sterility. Its lavish wealth stood in stark contrast to the destitution of the rest of the city.

Then Osi was inside that building. Below him, the floor was a grid of black-and-white squares; above, the soaring, pointed ceiling bore a hypnotic geometry of colored tile. Around him, there was a standoff— the tension of violence was a breath held to bursting.

On one side was a woman Osi immediately recognized as Oba

Ijefi, one of the City of Truth's historical heroes. Her hair was a cloud of white curls, her garb rich crimson silk, her wrists heavy with gold. She sat upon a throne that had been cut into a tree, and she had a row of red-clad guardsmen standing beside her in both directions, a semicircle of stoic faces and heavy spears.

On the other side, a small boy with big ears in shabby, dark cotton.

"Speaker, you have returned," Oba Ijefi said. Her smile didn't reach her eyes. "Have you found water?"

What is this? Osi thought. *How can that boy be the Speaker?*

"I found something better than water, my oba. I found the truth."

Oba Ijefi adjusted herself in her seat. The soldiers seemed to take that as a cue; there was a silent, subtle tensing, a readying for combat.

"Where is my mama?" the boy asked.

"Your mama," the oba said. Her eyes narrowed and her voice fell flat. "Your mama is dead. You did not know? Well, no matter."

She waved her hand the slightest bit and her guards leveled their spears, slowly approaching the boy.

"Goodbye, Speaker," she said.

The boy's skin began to sparkle and he stomped the ground, halting the advance of the guards. There was a deep and yawning groan in the floor of the palace, accompanied by the snaking sound of cracks opening. The floor suddenly collapsed inward, falling away in chunks of black and white.

It was a long silence before the first splash. Then there was a barrage of them, each chunk of floor issuing a *plunk* and *shoosh*. Osi looked down into the hole, where rippled a reservoir of crisp, cool water.

Not far from where Osi stood was a city choked dry by the desert, its people face-to-face with death. Yet here, trapped in the plateau beneath the palace, was enough water to slake the city's thirst for a dozen years. It was a cruelty Osi was unable to comprehend.

Yet it was familiar. Something about the entire scene bothered him the same way Obasa had—he didn't know how or why, but he recognized it.

"This," the boy said, "is the truth I learned."

Oba Ijefi scoffed. "And the truth you will die with." The guards readied themselves.

"I will not fight you, Oba Ijefi. I am only here to speak for my people."

"Good," she said. "May your people remember you truly, Tutu."

Tutu?

At a gesture from Oba Ijefi, one of the guards hefted his bronze spear and hurled it at Tutu. Tutu recoiled, sheltering his head. When the spear hit him, it rebounded—energy instantly absorbed and released—and flew back across the room.

Oba Ijefi didn't even have time to throw up her arms; her only reaction was a slight widening of the eyes. The spear had torn through her gut, shearing through organ and muscle and bone, driving even through the thick wooden throne behind her.

This is the Spearman, Osi realized.

He'd heard this story dozens of times. He'd told it himself just as many. But this wasn't right. Everything was jumbled.

Tutu stared in horror at his dead oba, too distraught to notice the guards had come upon him from behind. They skewered him upon their spears, ending the life of a boy who had done nothing wrong but protect himself and his people. He crumpled to the palace floor, blood in a crimson bloom around him.

Osi couldn't tell whether Tutu was looking at him or his dead eyes had simply fallen in Osi's direction, but somehow the connection of their eyes transmitted feeling. He felt the lengths of cold spear within him, the carved-up mangle of his innards, the steady, unnatural pump of his blood into the world. Most of all, he felt the boy's desire for a kinder world. And his regret that such a world had come too late for he and his mama to share.

Then the world went black again, and Osi was blinded by infinite knowledge until Obasa's hand left his head and he was returned to his bloodstained cell.

"Blood of Tutu," Osi swore though heavy breaths. Tears slid down his face, dripping from his chin. He wasn't certain whether they were his own or from the boy. From Tutu.

Obasa stepped away and his shining scales faded back to skin. "In those days," he said, "all oba deprived their people to maintain power. It was Tutu and his spear that changed everything. This is why we call ourselves the Spear of Tutu. We are no cult."

"What did you do to me?" Osi slurred. He felt like he'd been drowned and revived.

"I gave you the truth you were seeking."

The City of Lies. Oba Ijefi. The Spearman. But everything was wrong. That wasn't how things had happened.

"That was not . . ." he began, but he couldn't finish.

"Not what?" Obasa spoke softly, watching Osi with knowing, compassionate eyes. "Not the history you were told? History is only a story, told by those with power to justify why they have it. The truth does not bend to power's whims."

Osi wanted to name Obasa a liar, but he knew in each beat of his heart that what he'd seen was true. The memory of Tutu's pain still sat in him, as certain as the stump of his arm. Oba Ijefi was no peacemaker. Chief Tutu was no warlord.

Remember the Spearman.

There was no Spearman.

Obasa knocked on the door behind him. "Release the child," he said.

He strode toward Osi, fishing an iron key from his khaftan. "This old man honors his words," he said. One by one, he unlocked the shackles around Osi's wrist and legs.

Osi fell, his body touching the ground for the first time in what felt like months. But he did not move. The Truthseekers had betrayed him. Baba's wisdom had failed. The Spearman was a lie.

He no longer trusted his knowledge. He'd lost his conviction.

Obasa stepped back, returned the key to his khaftan, and sat cross-legged on the floor. "You are free to leave. But I imagine you have many questions."

Suddenly, the interrogator was gone. In his place was an earnest, and even lonely, old man. An old man who, like many old men, seemed desperate to share his stories with anyone who would listen.

"So you are also free to stay."

13

THERE WAS NO WATER in the Forever Desert.

There hadn't been for as long as any could remember. Once, a river had coursed through it, but then across the desert had come gold-robed killers, the Truthseekers, who butchered the people living along its banks and dammed it up so that its waters would only flow through their City of Lies. The Truthseekers had then offered to sell the water back to the people of the Forever Desert, but at a steeper price: tongues. The tongues of all their citizens, everyone thirteen years or older. It was a twofold price, a price of blood and a price of history: an untongued people cannot tell their story.

But neither could the dead.

So they paid the price, exchanging tongues for water year after year, decade after decade, century after century.

Then came the Aleke. With his Sight and his leadership, he was able to bring together warriors from across the Forever Desert to defend their lands. They called themselves the Spear of Tutu, warriors fighting in memory of the boy who defied the power of his time. They repelled the Truthseekers and raided the City of Lies, taking water by force and returning it to the people from whom it had been stolen. Thus began the war that would last generations and consume countless lives on both sides.

Obasa told Osi this story as they traveled upon camelback from the Sacrificial Tower—or Tower of Victory, Obasa said it was called. They were going back into the slums, where Obasa had offered Osi a home to stay in while his body healed. Along the ride, Osi asked question after question, hoping something would explain why Tutu's eyes refused to leave his memory.

"How do you do it?" Osi asked. "Go into the past."

"I do not go, young Osi. I look. I am a Seer, as are you."

"A Seer cannot do that."

"Is that so?" he said with an amused smile. "The Truthseekers convinced you of their lies, eh?"

Osi didn't respond. Every thought of the Truthseekers brought pain.

"In the days of Tutu," Obasa said. "Very few could See. One in a million, it was said. Now, it is far more. In your City of Lies, it seems everyone can See if given God's Eyes. Even here, it is not so rare as it once was. Do you think the Goddess has given us this power so we can kill each other? Do you not wonder why She punishes us when we hurt others?"

The price of the Seer. He'd been taught that it was the unavoidable cost of power, that the best course was to numb himself in order to overcome it.

"This power," Obasa continued, "is not a tool for killing. It is a tool for education. To learn about our world and its history so that we do not repeat the follies of the past. The day I understood this was the day I became as powerful as you see me now."

The Truthseekers taught that the power of Seeing came from one's knowledge of what is, driven through conviction in that knowledge. Perception was the best attribute for a Seer, and much of Truthseeker training forced a student to watch, listen, observe.

But Obasa thought differently. "From the study of what was," he said, "comes the knowledge of what is."

He spent his days in books, seeking out any pages that held stories of the past and reading them until he had them committed to memory. In his youth, he'd tried to use Sight as the Truthseekers did, for fighting. But he soon learned he had no appetite for punching and kicking and stabbing others.

"I find it hard to numb myself," Obasa said. He cleared his throat and stared ahead.

Osi thought back to that night in the iron shack and how easily the Truthseekers had ended a family. Even Lumhen, who he had once believed was of a better heart than the others, had shown no remorse.

"Me too," Osi muttered.

Obasa gave him a sideways look, then a sympathetic nod.

They rode on in comfortable silence.

After an hour of travel through hot, barren sand, they passed through the cramped and filthy slums. It was worse during the day. The people out on the streets were emaciated, cheeks as sharp against their skin as their ribs, and the gagging stench of feces and urine was ripened by the heat.

Their destination was a surprisingly modern residence, sealed up mud brick rather than the ramshackle half-iron constructions most of the people lived in. As they arrived, a giant of a man was exiting it, ducking beneath the doorway. He was young—not yet thirty—and his face was framed by a spill of short braids. Even without his moon-blade war scythe, even without his hippo armor, even without his head enclosed in his horned helm, Osi recognized him by his size, and by the lethal rage trapped within his eyes as soon as their gazes met.

The Aleke.

"Osi is our guest," Obasa cautioned, raising a staying hand. "We will not harm him."

Within Osi, the lies of his childhood warred with his newly learned truths. Whatever the Aleke was to the people of the Forever Desert, he was still the man who had orchestrated the Fall. He had taken Dikende's head, Osi's arm, and hundreds of innocent lives. Whether or not he was a Truthseeker anymore, Osi was still a citizen of the City of Truth, and the Aleke was still his enemy. It was his last chance to right so many wrongs.

But when he summoned his knowledge of the world, he found it lacking. And when he tried to reinforce it with conviction, he found himself empty.

He had no Sight.

Yet the Aleke did not move to attack. He tightened his meaty jaw, but he obeyed Obasa's command.

"Osi, this is my greatson I have told you about. His name is Bango. And he is no longer your enemy."

"Your greatson is the Aleke?" Osi asked.

Obasa's quizzical look transformed into a sudden roar of laughter, and beneath his mask of murderous rage, the Aleke looked suddenly embarrassed. "You think this empty-headed boy is the Aleke?" Obasa asked with a final heavy chuckle.

Osi looked between Obasa and the giant, confusion eating at his resolve.

"I thought you were perceptive, Osi." Obasa collected himself, drawing his posture upright with a presence and stateliness that had been previously hidden. "*I am the Aleke.*"

14

TRUTH IS A CRUEL TEACHER. It does not appease. It does not reconsider. Its lessons vary in delivery—sometimes trickling in over decades, sometimes crashing down all at once—but consistently disregard the desires of the student.

Osi had given his life to the death of the Aleke. A death that would not only solve the problems of the world but etch him in history's pages as a hero.

But the Aleke was an old man. Not death armored in night, not the villain that stalked him even in sleep, his presence melting dreams into nightmare. Just a greatbaba, one who liked peanuts and whistled old songs when he rode on camelback, fighting for the memory of a dead boy with innocent eyes.

The Aleke's home was a palace by comparison to the rest of the city, clean and sturdily built. Osi was watched over by a friend of Obasa's named Neni, a kind-faced woman in her middle years who seemed entirely unaware of herself. She laughed loudly, dressed nonsensically, and spent her days singing to herself as she painted portraits of the people who passed on the street in front of the house.

In the mornings, Osi stretched to regain motion in his stiff joints. In the afternoons, he sat by his window and watched the passersby on the street. In the evenings, he ate the food Neni left for him, then slept.

He learned that the Forever Desert was a decrepit place, full of desperate people. Worse, it was dry. Though it had been a long time since the days of exchanging tongues for water, and a few natural wells had been discovered, the region's water was rationed, and there was frequently too little to go around. Sitting by his window, he listened to the people talking; every few days, it seemed, someone died of "blood drought."

Osi had heard of the affliction before, but he'd never thought of it as something to worry about. Water wasn't rare in the City of Truth. Aside from the river, wells were plentiful, enough for each community to have its own. He wondered what it would feel like to die from something so simple, and an uncommon guilt whispered to him.

Neni seemed to be the exception to the water rations, sometimes drinking two or even three cups in a day and offering as many to Osi, and that was on top of meals that nearly rivaled the food of the Citadel. The nourishment helped to heal his body. His shattered teeth would never grow back, and he expected his hearing to be permanently damaged, but enough of his strength returned that he was able to exercise properly again. Eventually, he even felt well enough to leave his room during the day, which Neni took as a cue to swarm him with questions and affection that he ignored.

In his first foray beyond his new lodgings, he went for a walk. News of a former Truthseeker living in their midst had spread to the locals. His presence emptied streets. Playing children disappeared into their homes; blankets were raised to block open windows.

"All day people have been warning me," Neni said when he returned. The sky was pinkened from the setting sun, and Neni was out with her easel. "'There is a Truthseeker,' they sign. 'But he looks sick.'" She cackled. "So I knew it was you."

"Why are they afraid of me?" he asked.

"The boy speaks," she said, eyebrows raised. "I was thinking you lacked a tongue. I'd heard some of you Truthseekers cut out your own, you culty bunch." When he didn't reply to that, she added, "They fear because you are a Truthseeker."

He should have known. His own brief suffering at the hands of the Truthseekers was forgettable next to what these people had experienced. They didn't know he was one of them now, a victim of the City of Truth.

He was striding past Neni to reenter the house when he caught a glimpse of her painting. It depicted a small patch of desert-dusted street, with the body of a dead lizard smashed into the ground and largely covered by the sand. Just past her easel, the art was reflected in life, the same unfortunate lizard sprawled dead in the road.

"What is this?" he asked.

She halted her work and looked over her shoulder at him, eyebrows raised. "Silent for a month and now all we want is chat-chat."

"Never mind," he said. He turned back to the house.

"Do you know the story of the Great Gecko Funemi?" she called.

Osi's baba had been the storyteller. After he was gone, there was a lack of stories in his house. Osi missed them.

He slowed. "No," he said, waiting.

She set her palette and brushes down and beckoned him to sit on the ground. She turned her chair to face him and sat as well. "Long ago, before even the days of Tutu, there were three cities in the Forever Desert. These cities fought bitterly, each fighting the other as fiercely as brothers. Decades passed, thousands died, fathers and mothers fell on the battlefield, only to be replaced by their sons and daughters."

Osi didn't leave, but he was bored by this story. So far, it was just the story of a war, nothing special. All wars were passed down from parent to child.

"The fighting was so loud," Neni continued, "that it woke the Great Gecko Funemi from centuries of slumber. She was a giant of a lizard, a hundred times the length of a man, with a barbed tail so long that from a distance it looked as if a new mountain range had appeared. She was also a mama, and you know how mamas are when you wake them for no good reason."

Osi nodded. "So she killed all the humans?"

"Are we not human? If she killed all the humans, then who is speaking right now?" Neni asked.

Osi shrugged. He hadn't taken the story literally.

Neni sucked her teeth and continued. "So she fed the humans to her children. She stalked the desert, slaying all those who left their cities, be it a lone traveler or an army marching to war. She fed her victims to her millions of gecko children, little lizards just like you see here." She gestured over her shoulder to her painting.

Then she took a full-bellied sigh and her voice dampened, somber. "But you see, for all Funemi's might, she did not understand humans; she thought they were prey. Instead, the three cities joined together, sending their strongest warriors and mightiest armies to stalk and slay her. And so now Funemi is remembered as the lizard that brought humanity together, and anywhere one of these lizards is seen—a Funemi's gecko, they are called—it is killed as a remembrance of when all humans united to kill a lizard."

Osi was quiet for a long while, unsure what to say. "I see," he finally mumbled.

"No, you do not," Neni said with a quick burst of laughter. "But you are a sweet boy, despite your appearance." She rose from her chair and returned to her easel. "Go inside, food is ready. And we have a guest tonight."

"Who?" he asked as he pulled the door open.

* * *

It had been just over a month since Osi had seen Obasa. Though he wore a greater heaviness beneath his eyes than Osi remembered, he looked much the same, and his presence brought a surprising comfort. In Osi's new life in the Forever Desert, Obasa's thick brows and calm rasp were the oldest friends he had.

But he was still the Aleke, and there was still within Osi an inability to forgive the lifetimes of pain the man had caused.

"I have come to explain," Obasa said.

First, Obasa was an interrogator, cold and uncaring, devoted only to getting the answers he wanted. Then, a lonely old man in need of an ear to listen to his stories. Then, he revealed himself to be the Aleke, ruler of the Forever Desert, the source of three centuries of pain and death.

Now, Osi was seeing Obasa the diplomat, apologizing tactically, giving ground in hopes of reaching an agreement. Osi didn't understand how one man could carry so many shades, but he knew better than to express that.

Osi tore a piece of flatbread from the platter on the floor and tossed it into his mouth to justify his silence.

"I see the anger you hold for Bango," Obasa continued. "And it caused me to remember that though I protect my suffering people, I am myself the cause of suffering. I have my grievances with your city, yes. But I did not intend for so many innocents to die."

All Seers could use the energies of the world, he explained, but few could use the fabric of the world itself. Gathering that sand and hurling it across the Silence was an unprecedented feat, one the city couldn't possibly have predicted. Bango and his warriors were only there to retrieve the God's Eyes in the aftermath.

"Only two living Seers can use sand in such a way," he said, and Osi thought of Lumhen's fight against Bango, how she'd turned the sand around her into a weapon. "It took me months to prepare. I would not go to such lengths without cause: I truly believed I could eliminate your city's leadership in a single morning and end this war. But I failed." He rolled his wrists, palms up, helpless. "I missed the Citadel, and as a result we failed to take the God's Eyes. It seems I truly am getting old."

"You do not have the God's Eyes?" Osi asked.

Obasa showed his empty hands. "If we had them, do you think we would be here suffering? I would have an army training every night to erase your city from the pages of history."

Painfully, Osi revisited his memory of that day. The Peacekeepers surrounding the Ascendance. The meteor crashing toward them. Izen's skin sparkling and the meteor changing course, clipping only the front of the Citadel before crashing directly into the people in the plaza.

After that, but for the one that he himself had found, the God's Eyes were taken into the Temple of Ayé. When the Speaker had said they were stolen, he remembered his disbelief. But he hadn't listened to it.

"You did not miss," Osi said. "Izen moved it."

Obasa didn't seem surprised by that. "The shield of the City of Truth. I will be sure to eliminate her next time I attack. It appears I focus too much on your Lumhen."

The sound of Lumhen's name, a sound that had once been the most comforting in his life, was a stab in his heart. His skull thrummed anew with the pain of her kick.

"You still care for her." Obasa winced and looked away, as if stung by a memory. "Only because you still do not understand her. Bango is not my favorite greatchild for any reason but that he is my only greatchild left. Your Lumhen has more blood on her than any three Lights combined."

Lumhen and the Truthseekers and the City of Truth were not the heroes of history he'd been taught they were. Osi had understood this the moment he watched the life empty from Tutu's eyes. But just because they were wrong didn't make Obasa right.

"Is this what you came to explain?" Osi asked.

Obasa stared, then chuckled. "When I was young, I would grow so impatient with the meandering minds of my elders," he said, and Osi noticed a nervous tremble in his voice. "I believed then it was their age that made them ramble, but I see now it was their fear. The truth is . . . a terrifying thing to speak."

"Then come to me when—" Osi began, rising to his feet, but Obasa's words froze him.

"I need you to join me," Obasa said. "The Truthseekers are growing more aggressive in their attempts on my life, and if I do nothing, their success is an inevitability. When I am gone, the Spear of Tutu will be wiped away. They will kill every man, woman, and child, they will raze our structures, and they will poison our story the way they poisoned poor Tutu's.

"Our story cannot end this way," he hissed, resolute.

Then he was the old man again, and Osi came to accept that this Obasa—not the cold interrogator or the commanding Aleke or the somber peacemaker—was the true one. He was just an old man watching his power and life begin to fail him, terrified that the unfeeling winds of time would erase him and his people from history as footsteps from sand.

The fear of insignificance was a fear that Osi recognized.

A year prior, he'd devoted his life to the death of the Aleke. He had believed then that it was the right thing to do, to save lives and bring peace, to himself and others. It was what the Spearman would have done.

You think you are always right.

But he had knowledge now that he did not have then. And it was Tutu who had fought for a more just world, not the Spearman. Tutu was the hero.

So where before the right thing to do had been to kill the Aleke, now the right thing to do seemed to be to help the Aleke, to follow in Tutu's footsteps.

Maybe there was still a chance, Osi thought, to become a hero.

Spearman, guide me.

"What do you want from me?" he asked.

Obasa nodded, his face grateful. "In one year, I plan to attack the City of Lies, and I need someone to lead my Spearmen. I am too old to take to the field, and Bango is a warrior, not a commander. You know the city. You know the Truthseekers. With you, we can win this war and finally bring peace."

Osi shook his head, and he was happy to see that Obasa's disappointment seemed genuine—rather than the anger of failed deceit.

"I will not help you win this war," he said. "But I will help you bring peace."

15

AT OBASA'S REQUEST, Neni began introducing Osi to the community. Beside her, he was less of a danger, and soon everyone knew that the dilapidated figure following behind Neni was the former Truthseeker, Ambassador Osi—not quite as powerful as his old nickname, but one he felt suited him better. The Fall had already defined too much of his life. He preferred to be associated with cooperation and peace.

Eventually, Osi began to venture farther out from the house, receiving an immersive education in the land known as the Forever Desert. Everywhere he went, he encountered the effects of the Truthseekers. The malnourished, the disabled, and most horrifically, the ones struck by blood drought, their dry bodies crumpled in alleys among a menagerie of refuse. In the poorest area, known to the Cultists as Sunset Street because it was said that nothing could survive there after sunset, Osi had watched a child die of blood drought in its mother's arms. Moments later, the mother opened the child's wrist and drank from its veins. She looked directly at Osi as she did. The humiliation in her eyes shone alongside a feral desperation that Osi had to turn away from.

Over time, some of the young Cultists began following Osi on his jaunts. Intrigued by the captured Truthseeker who had been given free travel within their lands, they followed first from a suspicious distance, their hands flashing to each other—the people of the Forever Desert often spoke with their fingers rather than whispering, a habit passed down from their tongueless Greatmamas. Soon, though, they began walking alongside him, peppering him with questions about his previous life.

"Ambassador Osi, if I said sharp words to you, would you kill me?"

"Ambassador Osi, what does a river taste like?"

"Do you have a wife, Ambassador Osi?"

They were only a year or two younger than he was, but they treated him like an uncle. He must've looked it to them. One arm halved, teeth missing, limping and leathered by his years of patrolling and exercising under the sun's mirthless heat. He wondered whether his mama and sisters would even recognize him anymore.

Two months into Osi's stay at Neni's, Obasa returned for dinner, but this time he brought a game with him.

"It is called Move Water Move," he said.

The board was made of wood, a rare and expensive luxury in the Forever Desert. Three shallow bowls, each about the size of a hand, had been stuck together to form a triangle. There was a small center area filled with rough brown seeds, and each bowl was imprinted with a symbol of one of the game's three elements: the Rain, the River, and the Clouds. The goal was to roll the dice and add that number of seeds to the bowl for either your element or either of the other elements, but anytime a one was rolled, the board rotated, forcing each player to play a new element. The player who got their element to twenty-one seeds first was the winner.

"But you must think, Osi," Obasa explained. "What happens if you add all your seeds to your own bowl?"

"It is risky," Osi replied. "All those seeds may go to your enemy."

"Eh heh. But what happens if you give your seeds to yourself and your opponent equally?"

"Then . . ." Osi had to think about it. "You are vulnerable. Your enemy can keep all their seeds and win."

"So you see," Obasa said with a small smile.

Osi lost every time. No matter what he did, he felt like the dice worked in Obasa's favor, giving him the numbers he needed when he needed them and turning up ones whenever Osi was close to winning. He tried every strategy he could think of, but no difference was made. Move Water Move was not Osi's game.

Still, he enjoyed learning it, and he knew that meant he would do a lot more losing before the wins came.

"I wish Bango had your mind for this game," Obasa said one day, surveying the board before rolling. "The boy is built for moving bricks, not moving water. How is it between you two?"

Neither Osi nor Bango was interested in befriending the other, despite Obasa's insistence. Osi kept his distance, and he knew Bango did the same.

"Fine," Osi replied.

Obasa glanced up from the board with a skeptical gaze, then looked back to it. "You two will have to work together for the invasion."

"I said I would take no part in an attack on the city."

"I hoped you had changed your mind."

Their plan was to succeed where the Fall had failed—to steal the city's God's Eyes. Except Obasa wanted to invade after that, to kill the Speaker and the Truthseekers and allow new leadership to rise. To Osi, Obasa was an old man blinded by centuries of conflict. Even with the Truthseekers betraying him, Osi knew an invasion would only lead to more innocents killed. The people of the city weren't evil, any more than the people of the Forever Desert.

"I have not," Osi said. "We will find another way."

"So you have claimed," Obasa said as he placed his final seeds. "But you lose again, young Osi."

* * *

In the months that followed, Osi became as much a man of the Forever Desert as he had been a citizen of the City of Truth. He came to know the dusty streets and putrid smells. He could distinguish one ramshackle iron sheet home from another and knew the families that lived within them, could detail when the baba returned home from the mines or the mama ceased her tailoring for the day. As his health returned, he trained directly with the High Spearmen—Obasa's most trusted warriors, several of whom had been at the Fall—and Osi found them nearly the same as the Peacekeepers, an orderly bunch who took pride in defending their home.

The Forever Desert came to hold meaning for him in a way he never would have imagined, but in a way he was grateful for.

Over games of Move Water Move, Osi and Obasa continued to debate how best to end the war. Little ground was gained in either direction. Obasa still insisted on attacking the city, while Osi decided that taking the God's Eyes would be enough, and that it was something he could do alone. Then the Speaker would have no choice but to negotiate.

"Izen fights from the rear," Obasa explained, "which means she keeps her eyes ahead. From behind, she is vulnerable."

Rather than their usual meeting at what had become Neni's house, Obasa had invited Osi to join him at the Tower of Victory. They'd had to climb nearly two dozen sets of stairs to reach the top floor, where a view of the desert below rolled out before them.

"I will not kill Izen," Osi said for the hundredth time.

"Hizo is cunning," Obasa continued. "He hides it well, but he is poor at absorbing. Throw enough power at him and he can be broken."

"I will not kill Hizo."

"And Lumhen . . ." Obasa grunted. "That one . . ."

They reached his office door and pushed in.

Osi froze in the doorway, staring.

"She is more dust storm than woman," Obasa said. "But if you can wound her pride, you can weaken her. Then you can kill her."

In Obasa's office was the same wall the Speaker had in the Temple of Ayé. Rows of painted portraits, lifelike captures of figures through history, the same faces in the same order. The previous Speakers.

Except the last picture was different. Here, it was a woman with a small, round face, a shaved head, and heavy-lidded eyes. In the Speaker's room, it had been the balding man with the bushy eyebrows.

That man stood before him. He was older—bald now rather than balding—but Osi now understood why Obasa's face had been familiar to him.

"You were a Speaker," Osi breathed.

"Sit, Osi," Obasa responded.

Obasa said nothing as he pulled Move Water Move from a cabinet and set it up. They played several rolls, back and forth, in silence. Osi was stuck in a loop of thoughts, endlessly revisiting the same details of the past two years.

"I was the best Speaker in memory," Obasa finally said. "The Aleke in those days tried many times for a truce, but I was ambitious. I wanted to destroy her. I wanted to be the one history remembered."

He rolled a two. He divided his two seeds evenly—one for his own bowl, the Cloud, and one for the Rain. He handed the die to Osi.

"Your roll."

Osi wasn't paying attention to the game. He rolled and dumped all of his seeds into his bowl, the River.

"I pushed my Truthseekers too hard," Obasa admitted. "And in turn they pushed me into exile. See, the Light of the Truthseekers in those days was ambitious too, like your Lumhen. She didn't want to wait her turn, so when she saw that morale among the Truthseekers was low, she used that against me. I had done the exact same thing, and for the exact same reason, when I was Light."

He rolled. A six. Three in the Cloud, three in the Rain.

"I'd wanted to be a hero. That was why I became a Truthseeker. Why I became the Light. Why I took over as Speaker. So when I found myself here, bitter from the mutiny against me and seeing the suffering of these people—suffering that I was largely responsible for—it seemed like my last chance to do something worth remembering."

Osi rolled. Three. All in the River.

"Only when I got here did I realize I was walking the same path as all those who'd come before me, a cycle of destruction maintained by nothing but the certainty that in every era there will be individuals who can never be satisfied by the power they have. It is so simple. So unreasonable. Yet generation after generation, the cycle continues."

Improbably, Osi was one roll away from victory. He'd never been this close before.

Then Obasa rolled a one. They rotated the board. The River became neutral, Osi took over the Cloud, and Obasa the Rain. He'd been one seed away from victory; now he was seven.

"I know these people better than you can understand, Osi. I was one of them. They do not care about love or family or honor. They care only about victory. They will do anything—anything—to win. I know you have seen it."

He handed the die to Osi, whose mind was filled with competing images of Tutu's eyes and three bodies rotting under a blood-soaked blanket.

He rolled a five, added them all to his bowl, and handed the die back to Obasa.

"The Speaker has to die," Obasa said, rolling and adding his beads. "The Light has to die. I am an old man—my death will come soon.

Then everyone can start anew. We have sacrificed so many lives for war. Only when we sacrifice our own will there be peace."

Osi was on the cusp of victory again. He just needed a two or above. He rolled a one. Impossible.

Obasa rotated the game. Osi became the Rain, while Obasa took over the River, just one seed away from victory. All Osi's work was now to Obasa's benefit.

"Do you know why we play this game?" Obasa asked.

"I do not care."

"Because I am like them, Osi," he replied. "I like to win. And to teach you."

"It seems I am not learning."

"Not to teach you this game. To teach you about power."

Obasa rolled. Two. Game over.

16

OSI HAD ALWAYS THOUGHT of the desert between the city and the Aleke as a boundary. It was where the safe order of civilization ended and the wild chaos of the desert began. A year before, he'd stood at the head of a wagon in Truthseeker gold, bravely crossing from civilization into chaos to save his people.

But he knew better now. It was no boundary. It was a mirror. It didn't reveal a chaotic world, it reflected his own world back at him. All the evil and violence and oppression he'd believed were fermenting in the lands across the desert had been around him the whole time, more pervasive than he could've ever known.

He was again in Truthseeker gold. Neni had sewn up his old robes, extending the hems due to the few inches he'd grown over the year. The last time he'd worn this robe, he was standing in the front seat of a wagon, on a mission to kill the Aleke. Now, he was astride a modest camel, on a mission to save lives rather than end them.

Spearman, guide me. Spearman, protect me.

The trip seemed shorter this time. Before he knew it, the city materialized on the horizon. The gold statue of the Spearman gleamed in the afternoon sun; the Citadel's gray stone drank in the day; the homes and businesses welcomed him in their warm cascades of tan brick accented by the green fronds of the river palms and the hot plumage of tropical birds.

Osi started crying, of course. It was beautiful. But it was a beauty bought with blood, he now knew. Built upon a foundation of oppression, an oppression he had blindly helped to maintain.

He'd sworn to protect the city, and he would keep to his oath. Though not in the way he'd envisioned.

Soon, Osi reached the edge of the Desert Road, where an entire unit of Peacekeepers was already there to meet him. They were fully armed and armored, their spears ready. Osi brought his mount to a halt, breathing in the familiar scent of the river, wet and lively. The scent of home.

"Identify yourself," the commanding Peacekeeper called. His face was stern, focused, impetuous. He didn't recognize Osi. The Osi he knew didn't look so drawn, eyes so sunken, teeth missing. This man was a stranger. Possibly a harmless traveler, possibly an enemy powerful enough to rip through their entire troop with a firm blink. Yet still the commanding Peacekeeper stood, unwavering.

"It is me," Osi said. "Osi."

The commander raised an eyebrow, skeptical. Then the eyebrow fell, along with his mouth.

"Peacekeepers, stand down," he said, the order leaping cracked from his throat.

Osi hadn't been prepared for such an emotional reception. He'd forgotten that he'd left the city a hero.

* * *

"I forgot how much he cries . . ." one of the Peacekeepers mumbled as Osi stood before the Citadel of Truth with tears in his eyes.

It was smaller than he remembered—maybe seeing the vastness of the Forever Desert had changed his sense of scale—but it was still a place he'd called home for a year. The memories were still palpable.

"Do you need to go anywhere first?" the commanding officer asked.

"There is no time," Osi lied. "I have an urgent message for the Speaker."

He was led into the Citadel, where news of his return had already reached the staff. They lined the halls, staring with wonder. And horror. They recognized him, and he them, though he could no longer remember most of their names. But the boy they knew was gone. In his place was a man that was difficult to look upon, and some of them involuntarily pulled away as he strode past. Osi had grown accustomed to that reaction in the Forever Desert, but suffering it at home hurt in a new way.

Rather than going up the Citadel stairs to the Temple of Ayé, Osi was led along the ground floor to the Citadel jail.

"The Speaker will meet me here?" Osi asked.

The officer swallowed. "Apologies, Truthseeker Osi."

The sound of footsteps behind them made Osi turn. Dozens of Peacekeepers stood in the lone exit, tight against each other, swords drawn.

"What is all this?" Osi asked.

"It is a necessary precaution. You were a captive of the Aleke for a year."

Osi exhaled long and low as the Peacekeepers stared him down. These men and women weren't the enemy. They were good people, just being used for bad things.

"The Aleke is coming," Osi said. He kept eye contact with the officer.

A clear tremor of fear shot through the soldiers.

"When?" the commander asked.

"Within the hour."

"From where?"

"I must see the Speaker, please."

He sighed. "That is not a decision for me to make," he said, resigned.

He walked Osi into the cell, then stepped out and slid the lock into place. The cell was only a formality—there was no way brittle bronze bars could hold a trained Seer. It was the Peacekeepers guarding the exit that really held him captive. He would have to mow them down to escape, and they must have known he wouldn't.

The officer stared at Osi for a long while before stepping back, issuing a crisp salute, then turning on his heels and leaving the room, locking the heavy door behind him. With his Sight, Osi could sense the soldiers still standing just outside the door.

Osi exhaled for what felt like the first time since he entered the city.

"What do I do now?" he asked himself.

He assumed they would send Izen to question him. She was the most skilled in interrogation, and he had no doubt she would interrogate him as brutally as necessary. If he lied, she would know, but he would lie anyway. As long as they didn't know his real reason for being there, he could achieve his mission.

"Osi!"

After hours of silence, the sound was startling. But familiar.

"Inusu?" he replied.

She made sounds he couldn't hear.

"What?"

"I said, 'Are you deaf?' I have been screaming for you."

"I am sorry. My hearing is not so good."

"Not too loud! I am at the window."

There was a small, barred vent against the back wall of his cell, up near the high ceiling. He considered jumping up to it, but he worried the guards would hear. He kept still, lowered his voice.

"Why are you here?"

"I heard you had returned, so I had to come. I thought the Truth-seekers killed you."

"They tried," he said bitterly.

"Yet you are alive. I have so much to tell you, Osi."

"About what?"

He could hear the rising excitement in her voice—Inusu had always loved educating him.

"The Cultists—"

"Can speak," Osi finished. "They have tongues."

"Yes. And the Aleke—"

"I know it all, Inusu," he said.

"Of course . . ." she said. Then her tone softened. "Are you . . . are you fine, Osi?"

"I am."

"What happened? With you and the Aleke?"

"I was his guest," was all he said.

"You . . . his guest?"

Outside the jail door, there was a ripple of activity among the Peacekeepers. Something was happening.

"Stand back," he said. "I am going to break the wall."

He took hold of all he knew, reinforced it with his remaining conviction in that knowledge, and felt the clarity of Sight. He was hoping a more delicate option would present itself, but now was better than later. The Peacekeepers were distracted, arguing animatedly among themselves, several of them saluting their commanding officers and running deeper into the Citadel.

"No need," Inusu responded.

There was a loud crack in the air, then a throbbing from the cell's back wall. The area around the vent seemed to inhale and exhale sharply, and then a large chunk of it was pulled away. Daylight and the hot desert breeze poured in through the opening.

Osi climbed through the breach. Inusu was there, with a dozen uniformed Peacekeepers behind her who each held a length of a long, thick rope that was tied around the cell vent's bars. But not all of them looked like Peacekeepers. There were subtle differences—the brittle hair from a lifetime of dehydration; the tightness of their clamped jaws, as if they were afraid to speak; the clear discomfort at seeing Osi, likely their first time seeing a Truthseeker in the flesh.

Inusu held that same fear in her eyes, just for a moment. This fear had nothing to do with him being a Truthseeker, he realized. Did he really look so different?

"They are not citizens," he said, eyeing the strangers, trying his best to hide his missing teeth while he spoke.

"We are the Changemakers," Inusu said proudly. "Former Peacekeepers and people of the Forever Desert, working together. The uniforms are just for today, for safety."

Osi nodded to them, then took a moment to orient himself; they were outside the north side of the Citadel, desert stretching all around them. "I must go," he said, climbing down to the ground.

"The only place you must go is home. Your family is sick from missing you."

A heavy wave of guilt and longing washed over him. It would have been easier to go home. Better even. To apologize to his mama for being a fool and hug his sisters the way they deserved to be hugged.

But he had a mission to complete.

"I . . . must see the Speaker."

"Now? For what?"

"The Aleke is coming."

Inusu knew he wasn't telling the truth. Not all of it. She eyed him from the side, waiting for him to say more.

"We are coming with you," she eventually said.

"I do not think that is best."

She shook her head. "We have been fighting, Osi. The people of the Forever Desert want peace, just like we do, and we have given our lives to try to take control of the city and make that peace real."

It had taken Osi a year of training with the Truthseekers, then another year in the Forever Desert to learn what Inusu had learned on her own. She'd always been smarter than most.

Shouts leapt from within the Citadel, urgent voices calling out indecipherably. Something was indeed happening, and Osi was confident it was Obasa's distraction. Which meant it was time to act.

Osi set off.

Inusu and the Changemakers followed.

*   *   *

There was no need to sneak through the Citadel—the building was in chaos, swarms of Peacekeepers rushing in every direction, frantic to obey urgent commands from those they served. They made their way to and up the building's central staircase, emerging onto the reconstructed roof: a large square, at the far end of which was a small home painted to match the gray stones of the Citadel, but for its two heavy golden doors.

The Temple of Ayé.

Two years before, this exact place had been utter madness. Bodies strewn about, blood on the air, moans and moans and moans as hundreds of innocent people were forced out of existence. Now, it was peace. But only a temporary one. True, lasting peace would only come if Osi succeeded this day.

From far below, the shouts and commands of soldiers drifted up to him. He strode over to the roof's edge, where he could see Peacekeepers amassing at the foot of the building, preparing for the attack he'd led them to believe was imminent.

Inusu joined him, eyes scanning the growing forces on the ground. "Are you sure you do not wish to go home first, Osi? We do not know how this will end."

She was wrong. He knew exactly how it would end.

He turned away from the overlook and went to the Temple of Ayé. Just as he put his hand on the golden doors, Izen's voice sailed across the terrace.

"This is not a reunion I anticipated, Osi."

He sighed and turned to her.

Please, Izen, he thought.

She'd shaved her head and dyed the stubble silver; the look suited her. Other than that, she was much the same—thin frame, unslept eyes, not an ounce of mercy in her voice. Behind her were two Ascendants in crimson robes and a half dozen Juniors.

"Did you hope I had died?" Osi asked.

She shrugged. "I was fond of you as a comrade, Osi. However, changes in alliance are not historically uncommon."

She knew. Whether through perception or some other means, she knew why Osi was there.

"I do not want to fight you. I only want to see the Speaker."

She actually considered it for a moment. "I cannot allow it," she decided. "While I do not view you as a danger, orders have been given. You will surrender to me, and I will return you to your cell. Or I suppose this will be resolved with violence."

"Indeed, it will," Inusu said.

The Juniors behind Izen drew draggers and pounced on the Ascendants. The pale iron of their blades rose and fell, glinting in the sunlight until they were too coated in blood to shine at all. During the struggle, the Ascendants flickered with sparkles, fighting valiantly to repel their assassins with Sight. Several Juniors disengaged from the battle with holes in their bodies the size of fists, collapsing wide-eyed to the floor. But the fight was quick, and soon the Ascendants were still.

The Changemakers descended upon Izen, emboldened by the success of their comrades.

Inusu stood back in a position of command, watching her trap be sprung. As Izen disappeared beneath a cloud of pale blue violence, Inusu offered Osi a small, triumphant smile.

Osi couldn't smile back.

Inusu had no way of knowing Izen's capacity for violence. That her Sight was a hundredfold what the Ascendants possessed, and that the calm way Izen watched her Ascendants drown in blood wasn't the paralysis of shock but the cold curiosity of a child watching two beetles fight. Unlike Osi, Inusu had always been smart and brave in equal measure. But in that moment, her bravery overruled her intellect.

So Osi committed Inusu's confident and focused gaze to memory. If her bravery would cost her her life, the least Osi could do was remember her for it.

Then Izen struck.

17

IZEN SHREDDED THEM.

She walked forward, casually twirling her spear, mincing any Changemaker unfortunate enough to stand within reach or foolish enough to think she could be fought like a normal foe. They each parted like silk, organs spilling into steaming heaps upon the cold stone.

It was as Osi expected. As he feared.

But he had to do something.

Izen fights from the rear—Obasa's words swirled in his head—*which means she keeps her eyes ahead. From behind, she is vulnerable.*

Throat constricted, Osi inched his way around the edge of the terrace, rotating toward Izen's back.

Spearman, guide me. Spearman, protect me. Spearman, forgive me.

He recited the prayer frantically as he watched Inusu's allies fall, watched their iron blades be deflected and their determined sword hands sent spiraling in sprays of blood.

But then Izen staggered back, holding her cheek. An iron blow dart protruded from it.

Osi stared, stunned.

Inusu was already reloading the blow flute, ready to slay Izen the same way the High Spearman had slain Dikende.

But Izen was no Dikende.

With a single, wide swipe of her spear, she ended the lives of three Changemakers. Then she switched her grip for throwing, aiming it at Inusu.

Osi lunged. He latched himself onto Izen's back, his arms wrapping around her tightly, desperately. She shook lightly first, then began thrashing. He sank his few teeth into her shoulder, not to hurt her but to secure his grip, bracing against blast after blast of force from her Sight, his brain shaking nauseatingly in his skull.

Inusu appeared almost immediately, slashing at Izen's face. But even with Osi latched onto her, Izen's reflexes were sharp. She parried the first blow with her palm, losing three fingers to Inusu's blade, but knocking it out of her hand and off the Citadel roof.

"My back!" Osi shouted. Inusu immediately understood. As Izen tried to swing Osi off a final time, Inusu rolled behind them and reached into the back of Osi's waistband. There lay the iron dagger Obasa had given him before he left. A weapon Obasa had intended him to save for the Speaker.

Yet it was Izen who fell to it as Inusu drew the dagger and plunged it into Izen's ear.

Izen rarely raised her voice. She was always soft-spoken, even on the battlefield. Perhaps that was deliberate. Because in her final moments, Izen fell to her knees and unleashed a deep, raw, guttural roar, her life pumping out of her skull in a gradually diminishing fountain until neither blood nor woman remained in the body.

Osi dragged his legs away from Izen's corpse. But he couldn't drag his eyes. There was death again, that regular yet unwanted visitor. In life, Izen had been the shield of the Truthseekers, a bane of the Aleke. In death, she was a heap of bones in expensive fabric. All the training they'd done together, all her boundless knowledge, all her significance—erased by a few finger lengths of iron.

He would never grow used to the suddenness of that void.

"Osi . . ." Inusu was beside him then, arm bathed in blood. She slipped the gore-slick dagger back in Osi's waistband and rested her head on his shoulder. "We killed a Truthseeker."

She must have spent months recruiting Juniors in secret, allying with people from the Forever Desert, smuggling them into the ranks of the Peacekeepers. For her, it was the culmination of all her hard work and sacrifice.

For Osi, it was the death of a friend.

A *necessary sacrifice.*

Was this what Lumhen had meant?

"You hate them, truly?" Osi asked.

"The Truthseekers?"

He nodded, eyes still on Izen's remains.

"I hate all those who make people suffer."

A soft, slow groan sounded ahead of them. At first, Osi thought with hope that it had come from Izen. Maybe she was still alive and could be reasoned with.

But the groan wasn't from Izen, or any person.

The golden doors of the Temple of Ayé swung slowly inward, creaking on their mighty hinges. At the center of the opening stood Hizo. He was unarmed, clad in a nondescript black khaftan with coral beads around his wrists and neck. He wasn't at all dressed for battle, even though Peacekeepers continued to amass below for the city's defense.

Hizo casually took in the devastation around the plaza, eyes stopping at Izen's body. Osi remembered how hopelessly Hizo had screamed when Dikende died. This was different. There was a swallowed mourning, a pain internalized rather than released.

Then he turned to Osi.

"Osi the Unfortunate," he said. "Come, let us speak."

18

OBASA REACHED INTO his pocket and produced a second die, identical to the one they'd been playing with.

"Do you know why I will never trust your Truthseekers, young Osi?" he asked. "Because they are powerful. Many people liken power to a spear. Or an oba. But is it neither. Power is like water." He rolled the die. One. "It is not loyal. It is not honest. It has no desire but to grow." He rolled again. One. "Even when defeated, it simply changes shape or place, filling any vacuum it finds, persisting until the day it can resume its growth."

He rolled the die a third and final time. One.

"You cheated," Osi said.

"Says who?"

"Says I."

"Why would anyone listen to the story of a loser?"

"Because I am right."

"Right, eh?" Obasa seemed to mull that over. Then he said, curiously, "Why did your city want you killed?"

Osi's jaw clamped shut.

It was the question that had been sitting in his heart for the near year he'd spent in the Forever Desert.

A necessary sacrifice.

"Before you decide that we must negotiate with these people," Obasa said, rising and putting Move Water Move away, "ask them this question."

Osi thought long about Obasa's words. But he was still Osi, and he was still unable to understand what he needed to understand until it was too late.

* * *

*Hizo is cunning. He hides it well, but he is poor at absorbing. Throw
enough power at him and he can be broken.*

Hizo ordered Inusu to leave. She wanted to stand with Osi, but Osi
refused it. He was prepared to die, but he was not prepared to watch
Inusu die.

She briefly swept through the bodies of her fallen comrades, taking
small copper medallions from each of their pockets, perhaps badges
of some sort for their families.

She stopped at the top of the Citadel stairs. "They will not let you
leave alive, Osi."

"Nor you." One did not simply kill a Truthseeker and go unpun-
ished. She would have to fight her way out to survive.

"Then may you be remembered truly," Inusu prayed. Then she was
away, jostling down into the Citadel.

When she was gone, Hizo didn't lead Osi into the temple. Instead,
he just stepped aside and waited.

A woman emerged from the shadows of the large doors. Osi recognized everything about her except her scarred, emotionless face. And
he knew why that was.

"The Speaker . . ." he muttered. He had to fight the urge to salute.

Unmasked, she stopped ten strides from him, Hizo just ahead of
her. She took in the rooftop, also holding her gaze on Izen's body, then
sharing a wondering look with Hizo.

"Does Lumhen know?" she asked.

"Not yet," Hizo reported. "The Ascendants are looking for her."

"Good." Her eyes snapped from the aftermath of the battle to lock
on to Osi. "Yes, Osi?"

Even now, she was drunk on power, treating him as if he'd re-
quested an audience with her rather than made his way up there himself. "You ordered me killed," he said.

"Indeed. And you are here for revenge?"

"Not for myself," Osi said. This was the moment he had returned
for. "For all those you have kept afraid. All those whose children you
have killed, who you deprive of water. All those who died in this war
you refuse to end."

He drew the dagger.

"I learned many truths in these two years, Speaker." He now knew more than Hizo, maybe even more than this Speaker. He bolstered that with his conviction, conviction earned with blood. "I learned the truth of your Truthseekers, and the atrocities they have committed. The truth of the Speaker, the cycle of ambition that you play while others suffer." His skin blossomed with faint light, as much power as he could muster. "Most of all, I learned the truth of the Spearman. Just a boy named Tutu. Not Chief Tutu. Not a warlord. Not even from the Forever Desert. A boy whose only crime was speaking truth to the oba. He was killed for that. But he killed her first."

"Eh heh," the Speaker said. "And what else?"

"What else?" Osi felt blood rising to his face. "For three centuries, we have given our lives for the Speakers, and you have given us nothing but death and deception. The whole story—our entire history—is a lie!"

"Every story is a lie, Osi the Unintelligent," Hizo said. "That is why we call them stories." Hizo yawned. "The point is to pick *one* and live by it. Not jump to whatever story you enjoy this week like a godsblind donkey!" He pointed down, off the edge of the building. "Now look what we must face without Izen. I told you he was a waste of time, my Speaker. You and Lumhen."

Osi hadn't noticed that the sound of assembling soldiers had ceased. He looked down to the foot of the Citadel, where nearly a thousand Peacekeepers were formed up, spears, swords, and archers ready for battle.

In the distance, beneath a blackening sky, hundreds of Cultists marched in from the Forever Desert. Obasa had known the city would be on the defensive. He'd believed that the appearance of Spearmen on the horizon would force the Speaker to send out the Truthseekers, to avoid a repeat of the Fall. It was all a distraction, intended to leave the Speaker unprotected for Osi.

But Osi didn't want to kill anyone. He was done seeing people hurt.

"Hizo!" a voice boomed from the Citadel stairs. "Why is the Aleke outside our—Osi?"

He looked up into the face of Lumhen, glowing in gold, braid thick over her shoulder.

"Where have you been, Lumhen?" the Speaker asked.

"Meetings."

"Osi has returned," Hizo spat. "He and his friends killed Izen."

"Killed . . . Izen?"

Fear, sickness, regret. Each of those emotions passed across Lumhen's face, emotions Osi had never once seen in her before.

"Can we defend against the Aleke without her?" the Speaker asked.

They spoke among themselves, discussing strategies for defense while Osi listened.

All those lessons about power. All those conversations about Truthseekers and Speakers. All those nights spent playing Move Water Move. The goal was to fill only your bowl. But in any game, you knew you would end up playing for the other bowls at some point.

Obasa was right. It was a game to them. And all they cared about was winning.

"Obasa will not attack," he finally said. "Not if you agree to peace right now."

Hizo raised an eyebrow. "Obasa?"

"The name of the Aleke, previous Speaker of the City of Truth."

"Blood of Tutu . . ." Hizo swore. "Obasa is no man's true name. It is from a story. A story about . . ." He winced, raised a hand to his face, and rubbed the stress at the corners of his eyes. "Gods blind me and my Greatmamas. Osi the Unworthy, you are the king of fools."

"What are you saying?" Osi asked.

"I am saying you believed the lies of the enemy."

From the soles of his feet up to his chest, Osi began to fill with a warm horror. Something was wrong. *Everything* was wrong. He looked out again at Obasa's soldiers approaching from the desert. They were closer now, close enough that the Peacekeepers had turned their lines east to meet them. Close enough to see Bango leading them.

There was no need to send Bango for a distraction.

Osi rushed into the Temple of Ayé, across its checkered floor, into the Speaker's living space. He overturned the table, tossed aside bedsheets, ripped open drawers. He tore the room apart in search of the God's Eyes, but he found nothing. A part of him had known he wouldn't. But he'd hoped.

When he returned outside, they were still there on the edge of the Citadel, overlooking the impending battlefield. They hadn't even noticed he'd left.

"Why did you try to kill me?" Osi asked in a small voice.

The Speaker glanced at him irritably, then looked back out at where the Aleke's soldiers advanced. "Your death inspired hundreds to join the Peacekeepers. I had hoped it would be enough for when this day came. We will soon see."

A necessary sacrifice.

Then a cloud of silence descended on the City of Truth as the ground began to move.

* * *

Out in the darkened city, just beyond the Citadel plaza, the ground opened. A hole formed and gradually widened, swallowing every building on its lip, homes and businesses alike.

"Blood of Tutu," Hizo said, more prayer than curse.

The Peacekeepers below began reforming their ranks, turning so their lines faced the growing hole rather than the distant soldiers. Lumhen's skin sprang to life, illuminating the dark.

"It is Sight," she said, brows furrowed in confusion. "I can feel it, but . . ."

"What?" Hizo asked.

"It is too much. It is far too much, Hizo."

When the hole was wide enough for a half dozen wagons to ride into it side by side, it stopped growing.

And from within it a star rose.

It ascended calmly, lighting up the entire center of the city with its brightness. Only when it had fully emerged and come to a stop was Osi able to see the details within the glow. Fat scales of light, overlapping into armor. Head horned with light, hands alight with iridescent claws.

This was no distraction. This was real.

The Aleke is cruel.

From behind Obasa, dozens of soldiers poured forth from the hole: the High Spearmen. With each one, Osi felt a sickness in the depths of his belly as the portrait of Obasa's plan unfurled before him.

"I told you, Osi," Hizo said through a thick throat. "I told you to numb yourself, but you could not. Now Izen is dead and . . ." He trailed off, and his mouth set into a grim line of resignation. He, too, knew what was about to happen.

They all knew.

One by one, lighting up the city below, the High Spearmen of the Forever Desert began to sparkle. The light of their skin pressed back against the deepening night, the power of their Sight clear. Obasa truly had stolen the God's Eyes.

The Aleke is clever.

"If we survive this," the Speaker began, "the boy dies."

"Agreed," Lumhen said.

There was a time when Lumhen's callous dismissal of him would have hurt.

But Osi finally learned what Hizo had tried so long ago to teach him. What else was there to feel after being used and discarded? What else but numbness?

At a command from Obasa, the High Spearmen charged, and the terrified shouts of the Peacekeepers rose to the top of the Citadel. Panicked screams filled Osi's ears.

"The Aleke is coming!"

19

IT WASN'T A BATTLE; it was a massacre.

Obasa's soldiers were well trained in the tactics of the city's warriors, and they were heavily armed with iron. They cut through line after line of Peacekeepers until Lumhen and Hizo led a charge themselves. Hizo fell first, butchered by a mob of High Spearmen.

Lumhen raged her way to Bango, where the two fought for a second time. When Bango eventually took the head off a tired and overwhelmed Lumhen, the forces of the City of Truth froze; when he raised it into the air and roared in bloodstained fury, they crumbled.

The sack of the City of Truth would be remembered for centuries. Despite her strength, the Speaker was no match for Obasa and the Spearmen—he had her publicly executed before sunrise. The Peacekeepers were killed to the last, as well as any childless adults of fighting years. Parents were kept alive for labor but separated from their children, an insurance against revolt.

Osi watched it all from atop the Citadel. Each blow landed on the battlefield gouged out chunks of his spirit. Each citizen dragged from her home and executed wiped out swaths of his memory. When the battle was over, Obasa's men captured him, beat him soundly, and brought him to Obasa's chambers.

"Osi, the Last Truthseeker!" Obasa said, his arms spread wide in greeting. He'd taken the Temple of Ayé as his residence, its high, narrow ceiling above and black-and-white checkered floor below. He sat in a modest chair at the center of the room, the rows of portraits behind him bearing more an impression of mounted trophies than revered predecessors.

When Osi didn't respond, Obasa drew his arms in.

"My apologies, Osi," he said more somberly. "The intoxication of victory."

"What do you want from me?" Osi asked in a weary rasp.

Obasa's eyes fell, a heavy look. "You were instrumental in the deaths of many Spearmen. Their families want you dead, as do others. Your beheading is scheduled for three days from now, at sunrise."

Osi understood but didn't speak.

"But you know I am a kind old man," he continued, a twinkle in his eye. "So I have provided another way. A simple way.

"Join us."

He wanted a reaction to his performance. But Osi had none to give.

"You would not know this," he continued. "But there are many lands in the Forever Desert, lands I now intend to conquer. I suspect your fighting days are behind you, but I have need of those who will go to these lands and offer them my terms. Someone who can speak with passion, and someone who is willing to die should our enemies choose to reject our terms with violence."

Death now or death later: That was the choice Osi was given.

On the day of Osi's Ascendance, a twofold promise had been made: remembrance and vengeance. Since then, Osi had given his arm. He'd given most of his teeth and much of his hearing. He'd given his dreams over to nightmares and his conviction over to an endless doubt of everything he knew.

"You can become the Spearman you always wanted to be," Obasa said softly.

In the stories, the Spearman had grabbed a spear from a guard and killed Chief Tutu. In history, Tutu had used his Sight to deflect a spear and kill Oba Ijefi.

But there was no armed guard there for Osi. And he could no longer use Sight—he lacked all conviction. He would not have a hero's ending.

Instead, he would watch, wait, listen, and learn. In him was the memory of the City of Truth. In him was the seed of vengeance. If it took a year, or fifty years, then so be it. He owed it to his city, and to his family suffering in Obasa's prison, and to his younger self, that idealistic fool who had sacrificed so much for no gain.

"I will be your Spearman," Osi croaked.

Obasa sighed and tilted his head the slightest, relishing the victory. Then he looked upon Osi with an expression that so many had looked upon him with but that he only now understood to be deserved: pity.

"You were defeated by superior players, young Osi," he said. "No different from Move Water Move. Do not be ashamed. Instead, you must learn. The day will come when I am old, or sick, or my commanders betray me. Wait for that day and be ready.

"But for now, swear your oaths."

Osi sank down to his one good knee. He ran his tongue across the emptiness in his mouth. He scratched at the itch in his stump. This was the punishment, he supposed, for being a fool.

He bowed his head, hiding his face in case the tears came. But they didn't. And they never would again.

ACKNOWLEDGMENTS

I was in eighth grade when 9/11 happened. At the time, none of us knew it was 9/11. We knew the date, of course, but we didn't know it was the beginning of a new American mythology with its own heroes and villains and epic quests. In the years that followed, many Americans were radicalized against an enemy that we believed hated us simply for who we were. For our freedom. We soon learned that the enemy who hated us had more complex reasons for doing so, and many of us learned that our own side was also the enemy, demonizing us in the media, monitoring our places of worship, and a myriad of worse things. It was a cruel and chaotic time when the dichotomy of allies and enemies, of good and evil, ceased to make sense.

Osi is the product of such a world, and he made this a difficult book to write. In many ways, I believe Tutu is who I wish myself to be—someone who is searching for the truth and, when they find it, responds with power and action. Osi, however, is who I fear myself to be—someone who is searching for the truth so fervently that he can be easily manipulated by anyone who purports to have it. It took me a long time to accept the fact that Osi's journey does not sit as comfortably at the "intersection of fable and fantasy" as Tutu's. Because fables are often simple. Tutu has simple wants—water. Tutu has simple friends in Asilah, Lami, and Funme. Tutu faces the simple, inhuman evil of the Ajungo. Osi's desire for glory has more complex roots; he has multifaceted friends in Lumhen, Izen, and Hizo; he faces the more complicated and human evil of the Aleke.

But rest assured that there is no Forever Desert without this book. There were fuses lit in this book that are going to explode in book three. I am salivating; I am delirious with glee. In order to learn the final truth of the Forever Desert, you first had to learn the truth of the Aleke, and now that you finally have, we are all full speed ahead to a conclusion that I hope, in the most authorial and loving of ways, will dissolve you.

To my editors, Carl Engle-Laird and Matt Rusin, thank you for trusting me. As mentioned above, the process of this book was not easy. I imagine no editor is excited to see an email that the book is done but it sucks and needs to be substantially rewritten—multiply that times however many such emails I sent. But you both believed me capable of turning this into a worthy entrant for this series, and for that I am endlessly thankful. That same vein of thanks applies to Irene Gallo, Will Hinton, and Claire Eddy, publishers extraordinaire. And to my agent, Jim McCarthy, who has been there since the beginning.

A special thanks to the friends who read the truly unhinged early drafts and guided me toward this much more hinged final draft. Cade Hagen, my forever writing bro, who absolutely does not have time to read my rambling first drafts but always makes time anyway—thank you. Woody, Ananda, Alyssa, Rayn, Andre—thank you to the best writing group a boy could ask for.

Thanks to Alyssa Winans and Christine Foltzer for wrapping this book in a cover that stuns. The first time I saw it, I gasped, and I still gasp a little bit internally every time I look at it.

Thanks to production editor Dakota Griffin and to production manager Jackie Huber-Rodriguez for their flexibility with and tolerance of my delays. To my rock-star marketing team—Julia Bergen, Michael Dudding, and Sam Friedlander—and publicist Alexis Saarela: I honestly could not imagine my books being in any other hands. Thanks to copy editor Michelle Li, whose careful eye uplifts the story and whose enthusiasm for the story uplifts me. A similar thanks to proofreader Sara Thwaite and cold reader Madeline Grigg.

Lastly, thanks to you, the reader. To those of you entering the Forever Desert for the first time with this book, welcome—I have never understood starting a series with anything but the first book, but I wrote this series with you in mind, and I hope you enjoyed a complete reading experience. To those of you who are returning to the Forever Desert, thank you. Given how the last book ended, you all knew that we would be following a new story, so I appreciate you for trusting me to create a story you could connect with.

Until next time.